Notebook

Also by Tom Cox

Ring the Hill
Help the Witch
21st-Century Yokel
Close Encounters of the Furred Kind
The Good, The Bad and The Furry
Talk to the Tail
Under the Paw
Bring Me the Head of Sergio Garcia!
Nice Jumper

Notebook

Tom Cox

unbound

First published in 2021

Unbound
TC Group, Level 1 Devonshire House, One Mayfair Place
London, W1J 8AJ

www.unbound.com

© Tom Cox, 2021
Illustrations © Mick Cox and Jo Cox

Text Design by PDQ Digital Media Solutions Ltd

A CIP record for this book is available from the British Library

ISBN 978-1-78352-972-8 (trade hbk)
ISBN 978-1-80018-006-2 (ebook)

Printed in Great Britain by CPI Group, Croydon (UK)

1 3 5 7 9 8 6 4 2

Contents

INTRODUCTION

Someone stole my notebook. I blame the thief, but I also blame myself, and Michael Jackson. I was dancing to Michael Jackson's 'Don't Stop 'Til You Get Enough' – a song I can't ever not dance to, provided I am both alive and awake at the time – in a pub in Bristol when my notebook was stolen, and this accounts for my temporary neglect of the rucksack containing said notebook. Of the several bags left at the side of the dance floor in the pub, my rucksack was probably the oldest and least prepossessing – cheap, faded blue and grey canvas, purchased around seventeen years previously, and stained with the mud of many recent upland walks – so I can't imagine why the thief decided it was a choice that might lead to a brighter future. Having located my debit card, £46 in cash, my phone and my phone charger, he would surely have been disappointed with the remainder of what he found: a scented bath bar from Lush, a copy of Lindsay Clarke's 1989 novel *The Chymical Wedding*, some keys to a car that was perilously close to death, and a black Moleskine journal containing a stranger's chaotic thoughts on hens, garlic, second-hand vinyl, the landscape of the Peak District and Dartmoor, haircuts and cattle. The crime led to a fraught twenty-four hours: a sleepless night, the borrowing of cash from a kind friend, two long and nervous train journeys, immediately followed by a moderately confused two-hour walk in blistering heat and a very relieved car journey. But the pain of the loss of the money, card, car keys, bath bar, novel, phone – including the two years of photos stored solely on it – soon faded. The loss of the notebook, however, still stings nearly two years on, and will no doubt continue to, a little bit, forever.

So that is the first thing to say about this collection of jottings from the various notebooks I have kept over the last decade or so: there is a chunk missing. I don't think the notebook that was taken in Bristol was my best. If I'm honest, it was probably not even in the top five of the fifteen I've filled or part-filled since 2009, and aesthetically it was far from my favourite – I am not a big fan of Moleskine and tend to prefer fabric notebooks with floral or geometric designs, especially the kind Paperchase were making around 2008 – but it was still full of thoughts, many of which I will never get back; almost a year of them in total, stretching from autumn 2017 to the end of summer 2018. A couple of years prior to the theft of my notebook, I lost a quarter of an actual book in a data disaster on my geriatric laptop: a calamity which many people would assume was the more serious of the two. But it's the loss of that notebook that has caused the bigger heartache over time. What I lost of my book was arguably tighter and better for the rewriting and regathering that it prompted. That notebook, meanwhile, was a mess of half-completed thoughts, shopping lists, unexplained fortnight-long gaps and mud-stained almost-poetry.

Yet in my mind it attains more alluring mystery for every day it is gone, like an obscure, rare album that time and rareness is dusting with new magic. In my mind, I see it floating down an especially polluted stretch of the River Avon, where the thief has tossed it. It bumps up against a milk carton, then a hub cap, and for a moment the possibility looks very real that it could drift back to shore, trapped between the two objects, where it will be retrieved, its soggy pages peeled apart behind a warehouse by a delivery driver on a cigarette break, who by chance will see my appeal for its return on social media later that day. But then it is set free, and finally floats out of sight. It is at this moment, where the notebook's jet-black cover merges with the colour of the night and the oily water, that it begins to become much more interesting than it ever was when it was in my possession.

I have completed and published eleven real books – twelve if you include the strange little one you're holding in your hands right now – and I could argue to myself that filling the last page of a notebook feels like no less of an achievement. There's always so much temptation to abandon the notebook you're currently on for a younger, sexier notebook, in the hope that – no matter what your hard-earned notebook wisdom has told you – it might be The One. Sure, sex is great, but have you ever cracked open a new notebook and written something on the first page with a really nice pen? I'm massively anti wasting paper and massively pro beginning fresh notebooks, and it causes me to lead a very conflicted life. But I'm more disciplined than I once was. After I had my notebook stolen in Bristol and replaced my bank card, the first thing I did was go out and purchase a very pretty new notebook (the cover is the classic William Morris design 'Strawberry Thief'), resolving that I would keep it close to my person at all times and that it would be My Best

Notebook of All Time – a prophecy it went on to fulfil, holding the title jointly with a really psychedelic maroon-and-pink one I filled between mid-2009 and early 2011. The first entry ('August is the worst of all the months that don't occur in winter: it's scruffy, cramped and not quite sure what to do with itself.') was made on 20 August 2018, and the final one ('Story title: Impossible Carpet') happened on 30 March 2019. That might not seem very impressive for some speedier note writers, but for me it was a sustained, disciplined sprint, and constituted a new personal record.

It is surely no coincidence that the period of my career as an author which produced my most fulfilling work is also the period when I was a more diligent notebook keeper. What I have realised more and more is my notebooks contain the grain in the wood of my writing. Without them, it would probably be just a laminate floor. So many times, there have been sentences I have written on a keyboard I've been relatively pleased with, then later consigned to the cutting-room floor with a shake of the head. Equally often, there have been observations I've scrawled in a notebook, sitting on a boulder on a moor, and not really thought much of, then later, as a deadline approaches, been deeply thankful for. All books would be better if they could be written entirely during long walks, and notebooks are the bridge to making that closer to being possible. A lot of the writing in my notebooks ends up in my books, a lot of it doesn't deserve to end up anywhere outside of those notebooks, and a lot of it could have ended up in my books, but didn't belong there, for various reasons. It is the third category you will read here. I don't assume that everyone – or even most people – reading this has read my other recent books, but for those who have I have been as careful as possible to avoid repetition. This makes *Notebook* a different book to the one it would have been if I hadn't written those books, especially in terms of location. I have lived in four different parts of the UK in the last decade. There is a very large amount of Devon in my latest few books, a lot of Somerset, quite a lot of Peak District, but not so much Norfolk, yet I've spent five of the last eleven years living in Norfolk. Therefore, this book leans on Norfolk a little harder than on the other three regions.

*

What I see, going through my notebooks, is that I am more sporadic than I want to be but more reliable than I was. There are gaps in time, sometimes as much as a fortnight, which I can see are largely due to periods when I am constantly either asleep or in motion: days on end when I am either driving, walking, swimming, talking, cooking or typing the sentences of an actual book, and simply do not give myself chance to sit down for ten minutes with a pen. Maybe it is because I couldn't find a pen? Pens are the objects I lose more than any other, even socks. The notebooks contain some long-sustained, soul-searching bursts, usually written in pub gardens after walks, only just legible. Unsuccessful jokes are more prevalent in the earlier notebooks. My handwriting is often bad, but can be good when I want it to be, especially when I am writing in longhand regularly. This has always been the case, going right back to when I was a teen, and meticulously wrote the track listings to mixtapes I'd made for people I liked – usually even more neatly if the recipient was a girl I happened to be mooning over at the time. The first page of the notebook is always the neatest. Unless it's in biro. Biros *always* make my handwriting ugly, even if I'm at my most meticulous. There are also lots of bad drawings of hares. Malcolm Gladwell said that genius is just a matter of practising something for 10,000 hours. My drawings of hares are the exception to this rule. I have been doing them for a long time, and they haven't got any better.

The very fact I'm putting pen to paper makes me write in a very different way to the way I would if I was making notes on a screen. There's a more intense honesty to it. That's something common to this book: it all very much happened, often on the spur of the moment, frequently with a strong rush of feeling; it's all redolent of the real mess of life. Some of the thoughts and observations in it are better and deeper than others, but they are all real, and they sum up a moment, in a way a note on a screen never can. Paging through these old journals, I can still see the bit of river mud I smeared on a page in Devon in 2014, to mark the moment I started working on my eighth book; can still picture the weather that day, the way the pebbles felt under my feet as I waded across to a small island close to the opposite bank to write, the way my legs almost buckled due to the stealthy power of the current as I got halfway across. Reading some entries from 2009 and 2010, I get a better picture of the spaniel I borrowed for walks during that period: his smell, his lust for life – and death – (he really liked rolling on his back on top of roadkill). You look back at notebooks in a way you don't look back at documents saved on a laptop, just as you look back at real photos in an album in a way you will never look back at the photos you've saved on your hard drive.

There's an overused phrase nowadays which I dislike: 'making memories'. So many people claim to be doing it while in fact doing the opposite. In the big rush to make the memories, we lose so much: something special gets expressed in an email or text from a friend, but then digital time moves on, and it is deleted forever, whereas a few decades ago, it would have been preserved in ink then found in a box many years later, and pored over, yearned over, swam in.

Even though I've occasionally cringed in the process, I've enjoyed swimming in some of my older jottings while putting this book together, and cursed myself for not being a proper notebook keeper earlier in my life.

Many of the notebooks tail off into job lists and arcane unsubstantiated statements – 'People's faces... Wasp' – whose meanings have been lost to the whirlpool of time, before the notebook fades altogether, its final forty or so blank pages revealing the harsh truth: that I have abandoned it, once again, for the Thrill of the New. Within the pages, I get various reality checks about time. A story idea I thought I had in 2016 is actually two years older than that, which means, with a hard bump back to earth, I must come to terms with the fact it's even longer than I thought that I've been chickening out of writing it. But perhaps that's part of another lesson about time that notebooks – mine, at least – teach: that it might move forward in a linear, numerical fashion as it's happening, but when it's reappraised, it's actually all over the place. Some of the observations here from May 2015 quite clearly belong with some others from December 2019, and not with those who share their birthday month. A reminder I scrawled to myself in 2014 is far more relevant to my life now than it was then. A series of trips, or a habit, or hobby, begins in one month, but gets sidetracked, and resumes eight months later.

In my organisation of these thoughts, observations, conversations and micro-stories, I have kept this scrambling of time in mind. They do not take place in chronological order; they also have a bias towards my more recent notebooks, which are – to be frank – less drippy. The entries are dateless. This is not a diary, and it's certainly not a nature diary. If it was, it would probably be organised into

7

months or seasons of the year, like nearly all other nature diaries. My life is nowhere near that organised. There's nature here, but it's only part of the story, depending on what you define 'nature' as. This is a notebook, and it's as chaotic and erratic as a notebook should be. I felt any very clear attempt to organise into subject matter would detract from that. But there is a kind of order to it – albeit a freewheeling one – and a certain amount of editing. I don't want to bore anyone with the entirety of one of my actual notebooks, but I also want to retain, maybe even embolden, the customary rhythm of them. Each section covers a range of subjects, but to me has a feel, however scrambled, which unites the entries. I have always loved making mixes for music-loving friends, whether it was back in the days when to do so necessitated three hours with your finger hovering over the pause button on an old cassette player, or now, with the spoilsport assistance of modern technology. I have also loved naming these mixes, in an – not always successful – attempt to sum up their character. If I make a mix, it's rarely just of one genre of music; it encompasses several, but has a certain abstract coherence. After all, what genre doesn't bleed into another, or cross-fertilise it? And wouldn't music be so much more boring if it didn't? That's the way I think of the sections here: each is themed by nothing as strict as a 'genre' or 'subject', and the entries are often conceived in very different places, but they somehow belong together, even if it's only for the fact that they all came from my brain, and my brain, like most brains, rarely thinks about one thing at a time; it also likes to misbehave. In the end, that's what this is, as much as me writing an actual book: it's me having fun making another mixtape, for a slightly wider audience. If nothing else, it's a sure-fire way to make my handwriting as neat as possible.

IMPOSSIBLE CARPET

Walking through Newark with my dad, a motorbike roared past us. 'I KNOW THAT BLOKE: HE BUYS FISHCAKES AT THE MARKET EVERY FRIDAY,' he commented, before continuing his story, which was actually a story from his policeman friend at the swimming pool. The story was that the policeman friend had taken a statement from a student who'd been mugged at knifepoint in the part of Nottingham where my nan used to live and offered to pay the muggers with a cheque. The muggers declined and instead marched him back to his flat, which they proceeded to ransack.

'Going to write in a cafe' always sounds so attractive – even now, to me, as someone with a long history of failing to write in cafes. If madness is doing the same thing over and over again and expecting different results, anyone who had witnessed my attempts to write in cafes over the years would definitely conclude I was no longer sane. Somehow, when thinking about the prospect of writing in a cafe, my brain manages to edit out all the elements that so often make writing in a cafe impossible: the loud people who sit next to you whose conversation you can't tune out; the Tracy Chapman song that I vastly, irrationally dislike, which always seems to be playing in cafes, as if a barista is behind a curtain with a finger on the 'Play' button of a device, waiting for a signal from a colleague ('OK, he's sat down – hit it!'). Last week I tried to write in a cafe, but couldn't, so instead I drank my coffee, stared at a blank page and listened to one of the two loud conversations on either side of me. This involved three posh gym-dudes talking very earnestly and with great admiration about their newly gym-converted mate who wasn't around at present: 'He was, like, really narrow, and now he's like, really wide,' said one of the gym dudes. 'It's just, like, really great to see.' The two other gym dudes nodded in earnest agreement. I suspect all three would have considered me disappointingly narrow.

After two successive bank holidays, there is much confusion amongst the bins in my road about when they are meant to be attended to. One bin is in a tree. Another bin is crying. Several bins have left to seek work overseas.

The record my mum played most while I was in the womb was 'After the Gold Rush' by Neil Young. I heard it some more when I was a baby, then didn't hear it again until my late teens, when it helped rescue me from some other music I was trying too hard to like. When I play it now, which is often, it doesn't just sound like a record to me; it sounds like a place.

I want my autobiography to truly sum up my life so I'm going to call it: *The Reason You Can't Find Your Wallet is Because It's in Your Hand.*

*

You can write amazingly quickly for a big audience if you really have to. I've tried it. Whether the writing will be any good is another matter entirely. When I was reviewing a gig by a very well-known band or singer in my old job for a national newspaper, it was vital that my review reached the copytakers as soon after the gig as possible, so I'd scribble it down in longhand, make a few quick corrections, then phone in my appraisal of the gig to the paper's copytakers, who were based in Wakefield, West Yorkshire. I did this on an early mobile phone which my friends laughed at and called 'The Brick' and was originally just intended as a family phone for my mum, my dad and me to use in emergencies. This was never easy. On the way back from the Birmingham NEC, reception was very poor, and the route involved many tunnels and bridges, but somehow my appraisal of Puff Daddy's live performance was printed the next day and made some kind of sense. By now I was also fully aware of the paper's infamous knack for imaginative subbing errors. A mention I'd made of The Byrds albums *Fifth Dimension* and *Younger Than Yesterday* had been altered to create a little-known album by the sunshine pop group The Fifth Dimension, also called *Younger Than Yesterday*. I stated that Waylon Jennings wrote the theme tune to *The Dukes of Hazzard* and discovered the next day that the paper had decided it was actually written by Willie Nelson, despite the many facts suggesting otherwise, such as the fact that it wasn't. Tom Waits, the paper decided, starred not in Francis Ford Coppola's *Dracula*, as I'd claimed, but in Neil Jordan's *Interview with the Vampire*. Later, after being sent to review a rare and special Waits gig in Paris, I was particularly keen that the copytaker get all the spellings down correctly. 'That's Waits, W-a-i-t-s. You've definitely got that, haven't you?' I asked, then asked again, worried that I was sounding fussy. 'Yep. Got it,' said the copytaker. The next morning I rushed out to the newsagent to get the paper, in which I found a front page arts-section headline and review relating to a great gig in Paris by Tom Waites.

News from my mum: some squirrels have stolen the bulbs out of her best friend Jane's Christmas fairy lights and buried them in her garden.

Staying free: I feel, increasingly, that that's the most important thing. In time, you become better able to see the ways you could slip into not being free, but you need to be vigilant, because some of those ways are disguised as a greater freedom. Also, it's not that easy, even when you do very vividly see the actions that will make you free, and go all out and try to do it. There are so many barriers.

I always feel quite excited and liberated when I hear Kate Bush sing 'Take your shoes off and throw them in the lake', then I remember that I currently only have two pairs of shoes and that the lake closest to where I live is perilously deep.

The window cleaner arrived and I tried very hard to look like I was working. I don't know why. The window cleaner isn't my boss.

Al is over from the Czech Republic and has given up what he calls 'fetid vegetables': onions, garlics, shallots and leeks. This is in addition to alcohol, meat and dairy, all of which he quit consuming a while ago. He looks well and is infectiously enthusiastic about it all but it doesn't leave a lot left to work with. He remains a fizzy drink of a person, as charming and magnetic as he was the last time I saw him, seven and a half years ago, when he called out of the blue to announce he was midway through hitchhiking across the continent, then turned up five hours later at my front door in Norfolk with a black eye and his arm in a sling. He had, he explained, fallen off an Alp the previous weekend. This time we walk along the Ridgeway near Fyfield in Wiltshire, not all that far from his mum and dad's higgledy-piggledy home, past sarsen stones used during the Bronze Age to make hand axes. Armies of people once dragged sarsens from an ancient quarry here to build the pagan monuments at Avebury. Al tells me about the history book his dad has written about his parents' home village, a work of exhaustive research that took many years to complete. Once, a couple of centuries ago, Al and I worked in – for our callow years – vaguely prestigious jobs and went out a lot and drank the amount of beer that most men in their mid-twenties of that

era did, and sometimes more. Of our friend group, we were always the two people most keen to extend the night: him, because he was single and perennially excitable and in a big city, and me, because I found his company infectious and never didn't yearn to dance. He was always throwing himself off things and into things then, too: once, most perilously, from some scaffolding thirty feet above street level, onto the risky cushion of some full bin bags. In the daytime, I was interviewing my musical and cinematic heroes in my old newspaper job, and sometimes people still ask me what that life was like, but it's a bit hazy, almost humdrum in a way. Hotel rooms, a surprising burst of air guitar from a legend, PRs I'd never met before air-kissing my cheeks, a minidisc recorder I didn't trust. It's that image of Al during that period – his lust for life, his ability to talk to anyone, his habit of throwing himself randomly and spontaneously into the city's bagged-up rubbish – which remains by far the stronger memory.

What is lovely, when you're writing, is when a word pops into your head as the right one to use, yet you've never been totally sure of the word's meaning and nobody has ever explained it to you, then you look it up in the dictionary and the context is exactly correct.

Blackbirds and wood pigeons have taken over my garden recently, elbowing out the pheasants. The female blackbirds are confident and hang out in gangs of three or four. There's only one regular male, and he's much nervier. In all of nature, I don't think there can be a more perfect and exquisite advert for minimalism than the colour scheme of a male blackbird.

I have returned from my parents' house with around 3,000 homegrown courgettes, determined to use all of them. So far I have had courgette pasta, courgette soup, courgette stir-fry, and built a

small city out of courgettes. The smallest room in my house is still dominated by courgettes. 'You don't need to see in there,' I will say, in future, when giving friends a tour of my house. 'That's the Courgette Room.'

You get older, and your body hurts a bit more, but because you're more used to it hurting, it doesn't hurt as much. Sometimes you don't notice injuries until quite a long time after they've happened. You reach Bicester, travelling west, and belatedly realise part of your arm fell off in Market Harborough. You get drunk on an eighth of a pint of ale and the ensuing hangover lasts six or seven months. Hair starts to grow in some new places and stops growing in others. You develop a greater awareness of the crap most people are going through, all the time, and all of what you should be thankful for. You buy maps you don't need, notice the way tables have been built and want to swear when you sneeze, but in a good way. All this is true, and people might tell you about it. What people don't tell you about as often are the limitations that maturity places on spontaneity, even when you don't want it to. People have children to look after, mortgages and stupidly high rents to pay, health problems to manage; they're tired from working too hard; they are starting to wonder if it was the right decision after all to adopt seven dogs, but now are limited to the sole choice of living with the consequences. Just to survive, time must be blocked out carefully, far into the future. It means that reaching lunchtime one day and announcing, 'Guerrilla knitting party in the water meadow, 3 p.m.! Be there, and spread the word!' becomes impractical. I'm a pain in the arse to be friends with in some ways, as I still like to wake up on a lot of mornings and not really know what I'm doing and see where the day takes me, and that doesn't always fit particularly well with not being twenty-one anymore. I have loads of mates I can arrange to meet for a coffee or a beer or a film or a walk in a fortnight's time but nobody who is poised at any point to embark with me on a last-minute dancing tour of 1970s funk nights throughout the Western Hemisphere, which is a situation I constantly lament, but also implicitly understand and choose not to berate anyone but society for.

Such a beautiful evening here in Devon. Perfectly still air. Light birdsong. Pipistrelle bats beginning to emerge for their night's feeding. And in the wildflower meadow beyond, the inimitable call of young men on ketamine.

When I was writing big pieces for national newspapers, which I was often reminded were very important, what I often secretly fantasised about doing was waiting right until the very last moment in the production schedule that I could possibly submit them, and sending a Word document to my editor containing the words 'I want to DANCE!' and nothing else, then switching my phone off and going to do exactly that.

*

'Milly, don't go over there,' I heard a woman say to her daughter in the graveyard next to the shopping mall. 'You're standing on dead people.'

People don't raise the alarm enough when species of animal are declining, then suddenly the species is gone, and it's too late. But people can raise the alarm far too early when other things are declining, and forecast their extinction all too quickly: books, records, a type of chocolate bar. 'NOT MANY OF US LEFT,' my dad used to say to drivers who gave him right of way during the 1980s. But it is now the twenty-first century and, against the odds, drivers who give right of way still remain here, in the world.

I have woken up by the sea. Last night, I slept in the same bunk bed as the reggae legend Lee 'Scratch' Perry. He wasn't in it at the time. He'd used it back when he played a gig in the village where my friend lives earlier in the year. Apparently, like me, he was suffering from a heavy cold.

There was so much birdsong in Devon when I woke up by the sea, even though it was winter. Birdsong is something that can be a vital part of your well-being for years without you noticing or appreciating it, like having intact internal organs.

I like hats but they don't have to be expensive or fancy. I bought my favourite hat, which is made out of straw, for £3 at a car boot sale in Long Bennington, Lincolnshire, in spring 2009. It's got a huge hole in the front now, but I still live in it for large parts of every spring, summer and autumn. One summer I was wearing it when I went to look at a flat that was up for rent in North Somerset. 'I like your hat!' the estate agent who was showing me the flat told me. 'Thanks!' I said. 'Just a bit of a shame about this big hole in it.' The estate agent gave a nervous laugh. Back in the car, seeing my reflection in the rear-view mirror, I noticed I had the hat on backwards.

Sometimes you think, as an older person, you are developing a bad memory, but the truth is just that time is moving more quickly, and incidents are further in the past than you think. Your memory stretches as far back as it ever did, in terms of accuracy.

My dad was in hospital in Mansfield after falling out of a tree. He was given some pills with 'TTO' written on the bottle. 'WHAT DOES THAT STAND FOR?' he asked a nurse. 'To take 'ome,' said the nurse.

I don't think anybody should be nasty about somebody's appearance,

ever. I'm against it, one hundred per cent. Yet at the same time, thinking back to a couple of periods of my life, I can't help sometimes wondering, 'Could somebody not have taken me to one side and had a quiet word with me about how shit I was looking?'

A friend and I were in a cafe, nowhere special, and our conversation came around to the hair of a famous writer, for no significant reason, just the random, spontaneous flow of our thoughts. She didn't live nearby and neither did we. We looked out the window onto the street and the famous writer and her hair emerged from a taxi, as if summoned in an act of dark magic.

Never take advice from your mum on hair. Mums are mostly brilliant but when it comes to hair their sole mission is to sabotage your well-being. This is a hard lesson that you have to relearn several times, especially when, like me, you have a particularly great mum. My mum has cut my hair many times in the past, but if my mum had cut my hair the way she wanted to, my hair would have been very different. At my school in Nottinghamshire, almost all the boys got their hair cut by a man in town they called 'Mad George', for fifty pence. Having my hair cut by my mum, and not by Mad George, was one of the things that prompted some people at my school to call me 'posh', along with the fact that I had brown bread in my packed lunch, and wore imitation Doc Marten boots and dark socks instead of tasselled slip-ons with white socks. Since then, I have had my hair cut by proper barbers and hairdressers, sometimes for over £10, but I remain of the opinion that anything that happens to male hair that costs over £10 is entirely fictional.

My dad still has a good head of hair, at seventy. My mum's theory is that he has 'glued it on' by using so much gel spray. I timed how long my dad sprayed his hair once, and it was forty-two seconds. There was then a pause, and he began spraying again, for a further thirteen seconds.

'He's got curtains,' my friend Karina Dakin used to say, when talking about a boy she liked, in Nottinghamshire, where we both lived. After a while she didn't even need to say it; she'd just do a slicing motion with her hands below both ears. I always knew instantly what she meant. 1992 was sliding into 1993 and everyone wanted curtains. I couldn't have curtains because my hair was too thick and curly. I resented my curly hair and the way it seemed to resemble a vast straw mushroom every time I grew it. Curls are like large breasts in probably one way only: they're brilliant and a lot of people want them but frequently not the people who actually own them. These days, I am happy to be curly, wouldn't want it any other way and admire the way many young folk embrace their curls and let them fly, but the 1990s were not a good time to be young with thick, curly hair. One time, my pal Robin and I got chased across an industrial estate near Long Eaton by a couple of thugs in the dead of night. When they caught up with us, I asked them what their problem was. 'He wants to beat t'shit out o' you 'cause you got bushy hair,' said one of the thugs, pointing to his accomplice. This did not surprise me as much as you might imagine. It was that kind of place, and that kind of time.

I went for a haircut at a new place. After my haircut, the hairdresser fetched my duffle coat from the peg in the corner of the room. I'd been thinking about letting the duffle coat go for a couple of years, but hadn't quite been able to bring myself to do it. It was very old, and unusually heavy, and I saw the hairdresser's knees buckle an inch or two under its weight. 'Here is your carpet, sir!' he said, handing it to me.

*

It felt like irons were poised to be a much more important aspect of life, when I was growing up. Same with shoe polish. I've got an iron, but I haven't used it for ages, and I haven't applied any shoe polish to a shoe for even longer. Life has gone on, and nothing too horrific has happened as a direct result of my neglect. If you're diligent about ironing you might spend, say, thirteen hours of the next year ironing. You'll have neat clothes but remember the cost: that's thirteen hours you've lost that you could have used walking through haunted forests, visiting esoteric museums or befriending strange dogs.

My friend who works in a bookshop was in a bad mood. I asked why. She said her staff review of Edith Wharton's Pulitzer-winning 1920 book *The Age of Innocence* had been misplaced in front of Sophie Kinsella's bestselling 2004 chick-lit novel *Shopaholic and Sister*.

THE TEN STAGES OF BOOK WRITING:
1. Faffing.
2. Terror.
3. More faffing.
4. 'SHIT I AM SO BEHIND.'
5. Zombie who can't think about anything but book and dreams about book.
6. 'This is awful.'
7. 'This might be OK, and that faffing might actually have been of benefit.'
8. 'Hope I don't die before I'm done.'
9. 'DONE! Never doing that again.'
10. Write another book.

*

Someone told me to read a book by a very famous author that lots of other people were reading because if I did so it might give me more chance of finding out how to write books that appeal to a larger section of society and also allow me to conduct myself knowledgeably in conversations about the very famous author's work, so I would not appear a cultural outcast. I responded politely and vaguely, knowing I wouldn't read the book. It's not the very famous author's very famous status and the book's great popularity that makes me resistant to reading the book it's that the book does not hold any obvious or even unobvious appeal to me; and I am permanently very, very conscious of how many books exist. At any one point, there are two total numbers of books on the planet: eight, or several billion. There are the eight books that mainstream society tells you exist and the several billion books that actually exist. If I was going to read a book as a cultural gesture, which I am not, the cultural gesture would probably be a sympathetic one leaning in the direction of the several billion, and tending to assume the eight were probably doing OK without my help. Sometimes the fact that a lot of people are talking about a book means it's good; a lot of the time it just means a lot of people are talking about a book. I'm not going to read a book because it's popular and I'm not going to not read a book because it's popular. I'm going to read a book because I think I might like it.

In my experience, brainstorming never leads to the best book titles. The best book titles are handed to you by silent, invisible hands, from a magic nowhere place, without you doing any conscious thinking at all.

My recent dreams have been characterised by a series of baffling literary feuds between me and various entirely undeserving targets, mostly deceased. I knew the situation had got bad when I woke up one morning in the middle of telling A. A. Milne to get fucked.

It took me years of seeing all the heavily promoted 'big' books pushed to the fore in bookshop displays before I realised it didn't necessarily mean those books were always being repeatedly read and repeatedly loved; sometimes it just meant they were being bought. For a spell, I now realise, my books were designed by my former publishers to be bought, not loved. The publishers put covers I disliked on the books, in an attempt to get the books into supermarkets. The covers were misleading: they put a lot of people off who might have liked the books, but encouraged a lot of people who probably weren't going to like them to buy them. They were chosen on the basis that what matters is sales, not art or longevity. The last six years, and very particularly the last three years, have been very different for me. I do things stubbornly just for me, and am far more interested in writing a book I'm proud of than a book that sells a lot, and I have a publisher who understands that, and because they understand that, it means I take more care over my work. Ultimately it works out better for everyone which, when you think about it, is kind of ironic.

Roget's Thesaurus was one of the more pretentious domestically owned dinosaurs.

I was on stage talking to a crowd of people in Sheffield, and I asked them if they had any questions. 'Will you be honorary president of the South Yorkshire Weasel Sanctuary?' asked a man. 'Yes!' I answered, without thinking. I took a sip of water from my bottle, which was on the table next to me, next to a couple of other bottles of the same brand of water. 'Any more questions?' I asked. 'Yes,' said another man. 'Will you reimburse me for the bottle of water you just stole from me?'

There were a group of Hells Angels in my mum and dad's local town over the weekend. 'ARE YOU ALL OFF TO HAVE A FIGHT?' my dad asked one of them. The Hells Angels replied that they weren't; they were just going to get some chips.

TECHNICOLOUR HAYLOFT

'This is Rosa Bosom,' says Bruce Lacey, showing me into the living room of his chilly, cluttered Norfolk farmhouse and pointing towards a seven-foot robot with a tailor's dummy arms, a chest full of wires and large red lips. 'Her name stands for Radio Operated Simulated Actress Battery Operated Standby or Mains. I built her in 1965 and she's inspired by the Harrier Jump Jet. She was best man at my second wedding. She gave me the ring, blew confetti and played the bridal march.' Visiting Lacey is like visiting the lair of a lost Doctor Who that never quite made it into space. Rosa is one of three robots who currently reside with him, surrounded by old costumes, large amounts of taxidermy ('A lament,' says Lacey, who is a vegetarian) and ventriloquist's dummies. The other two are Clockface, who is made from a Victorian vacuum cleaner and a grandfather clock, and Electric Man Mark II, a hermaphrodite humanoid who wears a corset and formerly served as the target in the knife-throwing section of Bruce's cabaret show. Is Lacey an inventor? Sort of. A performance artist? Yes and no. A film-maker? Of sorts. 'For years, the media saw me as a joke,' he says. 'The art world saw me as a performer playing at being an artist, the theatre world saw me as an amateur. I see myself as beachcombing, not through the art world, but through all of life, making connections.' The overused description 'Zelig-like' really does apply to Lacey, who has lived numerous contrasting lives in his eighty-five years on the planet. His late 1950s musical comedy troupe The Alberts were the primary inspiration for The Bonzo Dog Band, and were briefly managed by Lenny Bruce. In the sixties, he played George Harrison's gardener in *Help!*, made props for Spike Milligan and Peter Sellers – 'a very insecure man' – and played practical jokes with John Lennon whilst filming *Not Only... But Also*. 'Do you play that?' I ask, pointing to a Turkish saz, hanging on the wall of his study. 'Yes, but it's broken,' he replies. 'Dick Lester, the director of *Help!*, chased me with it at a party and hit me on the head with it.' In 1969, Fairport Convention wrote a song about him called 'Mr Lacey'. 'It's true no one here understands now,' they sing. 'But maybe someday they'll catch up with you.' Lacey argues – showing me a banned Union Jack poster for one of his shows, predating the Sex Pistols' *God Save the Queen* artwork by over a decade – that he's not ahead of his time, it's just that he's 'of his time' and 'people lag behind'. 'In the sixties, I was already worried about the things we're worried about now: spare part surgery, food shortage, overpopulation. During the drought of 1976, at the Barsham Faire in Suffolk, Lacey simulated rain with ashes and cotton-wool balls filled with water. A thunderstorm ensued. 'Christians thought I was performing magic,' he says. 'I knew I hadn't but it excited me that I had got into a relationship with the elements.' A still more dramatic ritual occurred in 1982 when, heartbroken amidst his break-up with his second wife, he painted a seventy-foot woman on the ground at one of the old hippie fairs in Rougham, Norfolk, and symbolically made love to her using a corn dolly as a phallic symbol. 'Eight of my nine children were there, and my wife's lover was dancing and drumming for me,' he remembers. 'Art is psychotherapy for me.'

*

My friend Chloe, who lives in the Mendips, lost her hen. A neighbour telephoned to say the hen had been spotted at Wookey Hole, the subterranean tourist hotspot down the road, which, in addition to its world-famous caves and alleged witch, boasts such tourist attractions as a vintage penny arcade, an animatronic dinosaur valley and a pirate zap zone. By the time Chloe arrived, the hen had reached the crazy golf course, popularly known as Pirate Island. It was a busy bank holiday at the caves, and as Chloe chased the hen across the crazy golf course, lunging for the hen, and the hen repeatedly eluded her grasp, tourists attempted to get selfies with the hen. After much chasing between the holes – both those designed by nature, and those designed by the crazy golf course's architects – with little help from the tourists, Chloe caught the hen, and returned it to her garden, where two weeks later it was devoured by a fox.

I know you're supposed to do an excited coo over someone's new baby but I just can't. I am incapable of faking a coo over a new baby. Show me your new sheep or owl instead. Then I will offer a totally authentic coo.

I visited home. My dad, who had put on an old shirt my mum had been using as a painting rag, showed me the new wildlife pond he and my mum had been digging out, and said he was thinking of getting a rescue swan.

*

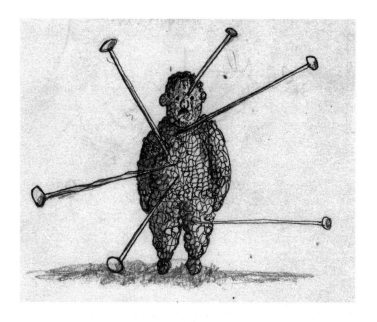

A friend met me at the pub and told me he had been clearing out his gran's house. One thing he'd found in the house was a knitted effigy of the man who had run off and abandoned my friend's pregnant aunt. Into the effigy had been stuck twenty knitting needles: one for every year since the man had vanished.

The general thinking in Devon was that if you had toothache, the best way to cure it was to bite a tooth out of a skull and carry it around in your pocket for a while. In 1833, Miss Elizabeth Greco, of an undisclosed village near Tavistock, remembered seeing several women and men in the local churchyard, earth, bones and soil all around them, tugging with their mouths at every tooth they could find. Toothache, it was said, was very common around Tavistock, due to the cider in the area being particularly acidic.

*

I discovered coffee at twenty-six. Before that, I thought it was something totally different: the thick instant stuff I'd bring my dad when I was a kid at weekends, so he could smell it then let it go tepid next to him while he painted pictures of cold Derbyshire sheep and cows. Now, it's my daytime work beer. It's also probably a large part of the reason I work best between 6 a.m. and 1 p.m. That's when I have to bottle the thoughts, before they're gone, because immediately after that I might as well not bother. I doubt I've ever written more than about nine decent words between 1 p.m. and 4 p.m. I can try to correct that with coffee, but it just doesn't work in the same way it does in the morning. 'He thought it was inspiration but it was just caffeine' wouldn't be the least fitting epitaph for me.

Growing up, I was warned a lot about the dangers of having no money, of all the bad things that could happen to you if you didn't work hard enough. What I wasn't warned about were the bad things that could happen to you if you worked too hard. There is a fear in me that comes from what I was told about money and work when I was young but from something ingrained over centuries, too: being from generation upon generation of people with not even a tiny cushion of wealth. I also remember what it felt like when it seemed like nobody was going to pay me to write anymore. So I sometimes push, because of the fear, and believe I'm Superman, that I can do three times as much as others do in a day, and I end up wearing myself out. But I view The Fear mostly as a positive thing. It lines my writing with something it wouldn't be lined with if I'd had a family I could turn to for money or came from a more middle-class background. But The Fear doesn't want me to be truly comfortable. It has a fear of that too. It just wants a modicum of freedom. I am not saying that writers from more affluent backgrounds aren't driven by a fear, but my fear is different, and it's a part of what has shaped my writing life. It has taken me a while to fully recognise that.

Browsing my notebook from the beginning of this year, I see I've made a bold, emphatic instruction to myself: 'PICK UP ALL HITCH-HIKERS!' Whenever I've given a lift to a hitch hiker in the past, it's always resulted in a few good stories, and broadened my outlook on the world in some small way. Eight months on from my resolution, though, I'm disappointed to realise I've not really carried it through. Almost all the hitch hikers I've seen this year have been going in the opposite direction to me, so today, when I spot a man on the Buckfastleigh slip road of the A38 with a cardboard sign saying 'M5 or nearby', I screech my car to a halt and wind down the window. The man looks almost like a caricature of a hitcher from the distant past: his cascading hair is grey and I can't easily get a handle on where it ends and his equally enormous beard begins. His face is so deeply lined, you could fit several small estuaries in it. He has bags all around him, and looks monumentally tired, aching for help. He looks like the kind of guy in whose company you could really enjoy listening to the first Crosby, Stills & Nash album. 'Where are you going?' he asks. 'Exeter,' I reply. 'Neh, no good for me, mate,' he says with a shrug, and wanders aloofly back to his spot on the verge. Exeter is two miles from the M5.

Modern cars get panicky about running out of petrol far too quickly. I miss the old tough-love attitude to petrol from cars: 'Oops. All gone. So what are you planning to do now?' Now I have a modern car with lots of electronic bits in it, I notice that it is also extremely needy, and riddled with unnecessary anxiety about countless topics.

All the same, I have no desire for a classic car. After all, I wouldn't get the pleasure of seeing how pretty it was, because I'd be in it. I once hired an early seventies VW campervan and immediately lost my spectacles through a hole in the floor beneath the pedals. It had no discernible second gear, and I banged my head around a dozen times over the course of three nights of sleeping in it. The cars my parents owned in the seventies and eighties were always breaking down, with the sole exception of a Morris Minor they bought for a tenner when I was a toddler. The worst were the three Morris Marinas they went through, which broke down constantly in the UK, but which, mysteriously, were as good as gold when my dad drove them from our house, in Nottinghamshire, to Italy, for four successive summers of camping near my uncle's family. Once, he did the journey all in one go, meaning we arrived earlier than expected and caused my relative Jason, who had just got his first job at a petrol station in Donoratico, to squirt four star down his leg in shock upon seeing us. My dad loved Italy, as it was a rare place where everyone was as loud as him and loved pepper sausage as much as he did. On a later journey there, without me, he joined in, uninvited, with a reconstruction of the Battle of Goito in Lombardy; an incident that still, well over a decade later, prompts my mum to shake her head in exasperation. 'It was so embarrassing,' she remembered. 'I kept losing him. The worst bit was when he joined in with one side – I'm not sure which – and shouted, "KILL THE BASTARDS!" then started rolling around in the street, clutching his chest, pretending to have been shot.'

One day, animals will permanently overrun our towns. Deer will cake Primark's changing rooms in shit. Goats will brawl on the bar in Wetherspoons, while owls roost in the crisps aisle in Tesco. Waitrose, however, will tend to stay largely empty, due to the excessive prices.

*

It must be great to drive an Audi when underbeings like me with a long peasant lineage obsequiously drive their normal cars into a wall to let you pass.

'I SAW A DRAGONFLY IN NOTTINGHAM CITY CENTRE THE OTHER DAY,' my dad tells me. 'IT WAS SITTING IN AN ALLEY BEHIND A BANJO-PLAYING BUSKER WHO WAS SWEARING AT A HOMELESS MAN WITH NO LEGS.'

In the nineties, to get to the good second-hand clothes shop in Nottingham you went down an alley, then up a narrow staircase almost completely wallpapered with gig flyers. There were two rooms at the top: the cheap room, and the almost-as-cheap room. There were always hundreds of badges on the counter, where a friendly bloke whose voice was Nottingham in all the best ways took your money. The almost-as-cheap room was where I got my flares – new flares, but made to original early 1970s patterns, in many different styles – because in my head 1996 wasn't 1996, it was 1972, just as in my head 2010 wasn't 2010, it was 1970, and in my head 2019 isn't 2019, it's 1968. In 1970, or 2010 as some people insisted on calling it, I went back to the shop after a gap of many years, but dismayingly it was full of skinny jeans. I then remembered one other shop that used to stock the flares, which was a long way away, up a big hill, right on the edge of the city. It was a stiflingly hot day but something deep inside of me that likes trousers was very determined and I walked up the hill to the other shop, and discovered it was still there, but it wasn't really a second-hand clothes shop anymore, more of a fancy-dress hire shop, full of cheap eighties crap and comedy wigs. Even so, I went in and something made me lift up some long coats on a rack in the back room, and what I discovered underneath them was ten pairs of the flares; possibly the last ten in existence, each priced at £10. I bought them all, even the ones that weren't in my size, and the shop knocked another £15 off. Over the next few months, I distributed the ones that didn't fit amongst appropriately sized seventies-clothes-loving friends, like some bellbottom fairy. The only ones in my size I didn't keep were a bright orange pair: a choice I now have some misgivings about.

During 1997 my dad was on the phone a lot for work and I was too, and I was twenty-one and had gone back to live at home for a while, so I decided to get an extra phone-line in my bedroom, where I could conduct phone interviews with American bands for newspapers and music magazines. As soon as the number was active, I received a call on it from a man asking if I could book him in for a haircut. I gave him the 9.25 slot, owing to the fact I'd had a cancellation.

For a long time during his childhood, my dad believed that leopards didn't have bones, because that's what his dad told him. They were at the zoo at the time, in Blackpool, which was also the town where my dad's Uncle Ken got his Alsatian, Bruce, who my dad often believed was intent on killing him. 'NOBODY WALKED THEIR DOG BACK THEN. YOU JUST LET YOUR DOG OUT,' my dad recalled. 'THERE WAS DOG SHIT EVERYWHERE. JENNIFER WOODBURN SLIPPED ON BRUCE'S AND BROKE HER LEG.' Ken went to Blackpool often, and stayed with a landlady, which to my dad sounded very exotic, and made him hope that he too, at some point in his life, would get to meet a landlady.

'I will probably pop into Candlesock for lunch on the way to Derbyshire, if that's OK?' I said to my mum. 'What's Candlesock?'

she asked. 'It's the old Saxon name for your village,' I told her. 'I looked it up.' A small river weaves mildly through Candlesock and as you walk along its mild banks, you might mistake it for a place where only mild people have ever lived, giving rise to events that are exclusively mild. But that's not true. Once, the houses close to the river in the centre of the village were shops. One mistakenly once sold laudanum instead of tincture of rhubarb. It killed a man in the village. In retaliation the man's son broke into the shopkeeper's house and murdered her in her bed. On the west side of the village, the river hides for a couple of hundred yards in a corridor of trees, whose branches, when they have fallen in strong winds, have often been dragged by my dad to my parents' shed then used as firewood. You walk across the field from here and reach my parents' garden, where you will frequently find my dad burning garden waste or making friends with dog walkers and asking for their life stories. Sometimes, he will be wearing a high-visibility jacket. He tends to favour bold colours, as he does not want to turn into what he calls 'AN OLD BEIGE PENSIONER'. He recently showed me a mustard jumper he was wearing. 'LOOK!' he said. 'THEY'RE MAKING CLOTHES IN ALL SORTS OF GREAT COLOURS NOWADAYS. NOT LIKE ALL THOSE BORING BLUES AND GREYS AND BLACKS.' I pointed out that those were the colours I usually wear. 'YEAH,' he said. 'THAT'S WHAT I MEAN. RUBBISH.'

Cows were like, 'What are you doing in our field?' and I was like, 'Well, it's actually a public footpath. It says so over there, on a sign.' And cows were like, 'We don't do signs.' And I was like, 'Well, if you want extra evidence, it's in my AA walking guide, just here, where it tells me to strike across the field.' And cows were like, 'I never know why they write that. It sounds overdramatic.'

And I was like, 'I know. "Walk diagonally" would be fine.' And cows were like, 'Anyway, don't try to distract us. Let's get back to the main topic. You're not allowed in here.' And I was like, 'I am, and I'm walking.' And cows were like, 'OK, we're charging. Geoff will go first, because she's huge. So you better watch out.' And I was like, 'What kind of cow calls herself Geoff?' And cows were like, 'Geoff. That's who. And don't fucking mess with her.' And I was like, 'OK, no need to get aggressive. I'll find another way to the village.' And cows were like, 'Yeah, you will.' And I was like, 'I will. I'm leaving. Right now.' And cows were like, 'No you're not. You're passing very slowly around the edge of the field, giving the impression that you're leaving, but actually sneakily working towards your original destination.' And I was like, 'Yeah, I am. What are you going to do about it?' And cows were like, 'Well, nothing actually, because for reasons known only to ourselves we find that kind of movement less of a cause for concern.' And then all fourteen of us resumed our business of the day, without further debate.

URBAN BLUEGRASS

A lot of people have now died. That much is clear. John Barker, the steam-circus proprietor, was crushed between two wagons at the original Norwich Cattle Market in 1897 while setting up a steam roundabout. He suffered fractures to the spine and breastbone, punctures to both lungs, and broke fourteen ribs, which is at least a couple of ribs more than I had thought humans had in their bodies until just now when I read about it. A renowned campaigner for travellers' rights, he was survived by a wife – although only for three more years – and fifteen children. There's nearly always a squirrel or three playing up near Barker's stone bust, which is perched on a small plinth in the Rosary Cemetery on a stationary stone carousel which seems to suggest that, were you to insert an old coin into it, his carved industrial face might come alive and speak to you, offering one fact about Victorian circuses for each halfpenny proffered. On recent walks through the cemetery, I've seen a white cat and a black cat close by Barker's stone head, the black one scuttling off yesterday in embarrassment after being witnessed unsuccessfully attempting a leap from one gravestone to another. Norwich's cemeteries are at their most poignant and beckoning in autumn, as their long green avenues begin to rust, reminding me of the way everything keeps rolling over, and will do forever, and my part in it. I cut through the one on Dereham Road on the way to hunt for old Viragos in the Amnesty bookshop and it never seems to end, and I think, 'Surely this should be enough for one small city? Surely no more people than this have died over the years?' Then I remember the other cemeteries: Earlham, Bowthorpe, all the others, the little ones, and the bones under the bones, piled up underground, altering the terrain. Two friends of mine went for a run here recently, then one had to stop and have a cry, quite understandably, because, as everyone who has tried it knows, running is very upsetting. A workmate of the other friend watched her cry from a bush, where he had been hiding in order to get the best possible photograph of a fox. He remained in the bush, silent, feeling that was the most socially acceptable course of action, and did not reveal he had witnessed the crying until the following day, at work.

I strolled along Gentleman's Walk in Norwich on a morning just after Christmas, and mostly people were just shopping, and drinking the dark liquid from Starbucks that some folk insist on calling coffee, but if you had peeled the big commercial sticker off the surface of the street, you'd have seen a fair bit of far more interesting stuff going on. A teenager busker was, delightfully, attempting to keep enough of an ecstatic grin off his face to enable him to continue to play his saxophone as a man with Down's syndrome danced to his version of a famous Dave Brubeck song. A few yards further on, a drunk homeless woman told a rubbish collector how amazingly skilful he was at picking up rubbish. 'You have to be!' he replied.

'You never know what goodies you'll find.' Nearby, I was drawn like a snake charmer's serpent to the irresistible chords of 'Heart Full of Soul' by the Yardbirds, which was coming out of the portable stereo owned by David Perry, better known as the Norwich Puppet Man. The Puppet Man waggled his not massively clean-looking puppets vaguely in time to Jimmy Page's guitar, waved them in the faces of the occasional pedestrian and did something which was not quite singing or miming. The Puppet Man will be seventy-eight in a few weeks, but continues to perform in Norwich or Great Yarmouth almost every day, as he has since the early 1990s. He announced his retirement over ten years ago in the local media, not long after gaining employment as a dancer at a nightclub on Norwich's Prince of Wales Road, but was soon back in his main spot, and presumably will continue to sing-mime for as long as he is able to. His puppets include Roy Waller – named after the late, not totally un-Partridge-like BBC Norfolk DJ Roy Waller – and Gary Lemon, who it is said is named after the Puppet Man's best friend Gary, who likes lemons.

I bought a slice of cake at a coffee shop, and a bag of posh coffee that I couldn't logically afford – a coffee that is so far away from Starbucks coffee, Starbucks coffee might as well be pork, or a pen, compared to it. 'Call it eight pounds, my dude,' said the laid-back guy who runs the coffee shop. 'Aw, thanks!' I said, not really knowing exactly how much he'd knocked off the bill, but grateful for his generosity and that there are such kind, laid-back people running independent businesses. I looked again at the advertised prices of the cake and the posh coffee. They came to precisely eight pounds.

Sunday morning. A brief break in what has felt like six or seven years of rain. The city semi-deserted, a different ambience to some Sundays, like the dregs in the bottom of an alcopop bottle six or seven strangers took sips from the night before. A walk to the University of East Anglia: a place where a brave future that never happened still looks so architecturally thrilling you start to believe in it all over again. A place where concrete is a solid, redoubtable promise, where you just want to get inside the concrete and lose yourself in learning forever and forget the rest. Hungover students milling about in kitchens in the Ziggurats, striving to locate cheddar and coffee and paracetamol. Water cascading efficiently down the terraces from satisfying v-shaped drains, which poke out of the building like guns from a robot outlaw's hideout. I noticed the Ziggurats – designed by Denys Lasdun in the mid-sixties – before, noticed them hard, but never properly noticed Lasdun's drains. Are the freshers in the picture windows aware of what a wonderful building they live in, or will that you-don't-know-what-you've-got-til-it's-gone sensation hit them in twelve, thirteen years? 'I never realised it at the time, but it really hits home a lot more, now that I'm living in a house with very ordinary and unimaginative drains, that those drains on my old student digs were really fucking amazing and enhanced my aesthetic life.' 2032. That's really not far away. I hope to have learned a lot more by then, and read at least another 1,350 books. But, knowing from experience the way it tends to pan out, I'll probably only manage half that figure at best.

I drove slowly past some hard-looking youths. It was a long time ago, outside the city's boundary. I don't know why I remember it. The youths were just standing about, not doing much. Spitting. Kicking stuff. They gave me a look. I am pretty sure what the look meant was 'I wish I was also in that Toyota Yaris, listening to Steely Dan.'

I would be a different writer if I had never moved away from Norfolk and Norwich, and a different person, which is really saying precisely the same thing, when you're me. Five and a half years in the West Country gave me a whole different set of colours to work with. I can't imagine where or who I'd be without that. I've noticed that my time there has tuned me into my surroundings here in a way I wasn't before. I notice alleys I never noticed before, atmospheres, doors, gates, seamless architectural meetings of old and new and less new that isn't quite old. There seem to be more churches than there used to be. The dust of the city's religious past blows down the streets in a way it doesn't in Exeter or Plymouth or Bristol.

The best way to find a church in Norwich is generally to walk seven or eight yards from the church you're already standing next to.

I watched a documentary about Norwich, the way it used to be. 'Chapelfield Road was home to an asylum for local women who had deviated from the path of virtue,' the documentary said. 'It was normally full.' There's a lot of city wall left, but it's in bits, so the city doesn't brag about it, unlike some other very old cities, such as York. Chapelfield Road still has a good unbroken stretch of wall, though. A long time ago, but not long enough for the city walls to still be fully standing, I went to get my computer mended in one of the tower blocks on the opposite side of the road. As I climbed an open-air brutalist stairwell then crept along a dark corridor reeking of piss, I became certain that I'd got the wrong address, but I hadn't. The computer was mended in a matter of hours. Now I cross to the other side of the carriageway, through the gardens, close to what used to be a Mexican restaurant where the burritos tasted of rubber. A man walks past me. 'And now we've got the kitchen we always wanted,' he tells his friend.

Autumn was ending and the Dead Time was beginning so I went on the Norwich Ghost Walk. I hadn't been on it since the very early part of this decade, and it's changed a bit since then. It used to be hosted by a driving instructor called The Man in Black. The first time I went on the walk, a friend invited a couple of women who turned up on cocaine and ended up offering to pay one of the monsters who jumped out at us by the river £20 to 'fuck off'. There were about eighteen people there, and one was a wino who'd just tagged along halfway through, uninvited. By contrast, this time there were around 100 people waiting for the tour to begin outside the Adam and Eve pub, each of whom – with the exception of the pub's resident ghost, Sam – had paid £8 for their ticket for tonight, which was one of three tours, all with different hosts guiding their crowd through a different part of the city. Tonight's ghostly guide called himself Le Morte and whisked us camply and authoritatively around the cathedral grounds, Elm Hill ('More

Tudor buildings are on this street than in the whole of London,'
we learned) and Tombland, telling tales of spectral underground
horses and a gruesome Victorian murder which involved a husband
hacking up his wife's limbs and distributing them around the
city, where they were found by nascent dog walkers. There were
no monsters jumping out at us this time, and the tour was as
historically interesting as it was supernatural (I had never realised
that the lavender still decorating the plague pits in Tombland was
used to cover up the smell of rotting bodies). Later, changed out
of his cowl and back into a comfy-looking tracksuit top in the bar
of the Adam and Eve, Le Morte told me and my friend Fiona he'd
only got the job a couple of weeks ago, which perhaps accounts
for what I thought had been a slight flash of unintended terror
in one of his eyes when he had taken in the size and raucousness
of tonight's gathering. He had done very well, despite being let
down by his habit of slipping into a Geordie accent any time he
spoke in the voice of a resident of Olde Norwich, but he had the
luxury of being in a good place for his trade: a city where stories
tripped over each other, just like in any townscape where alleys and
ancient doorways are rife. As I left the pub a light fog was coming
up outside, making the street lamps look like they were covered in
the hot breath of something unseen, and the season was palpably
turning over, squeezing the day into a brief wedge of light.

Walking at Cley next the Sea, in that washed-out light you only
get in Norfolk in winter: a sky of over-thinned paint. A Sunday.
Reed cutters on the marshes. Beyond the eighteenth-century
windmill, the coast path was like a six-lane people motorway,
but inland, the flinty footpaths between the houses were quiet,
and full of architectural surprises. The front of the old post office
here was built from the ground-up bones of cattle and horses.

We called these narrow paths between houses jitties or twitchells where I grew up, on the Nottinghamshire–Derbyshire border, in Sussex they call them twittens, and my Yorkshire friends call them gunnels, but here they're more commonly known as ginnels. 'Beware of the Bear!' announced a sign down one, adding more intrigue to an already very intriguing wooden door in a garden wall. Is there anything more enticing than a wooden door in a garden wall?

Message from my dad: WHEN DID YOU ORIGINALLY MOVE TO NORFOLK?
Me: October 2001.
Him: THANKS. I'M TRYING TO PUT A DATE ON ALL MY CLOTHES.

Few metropolitan places are as Red or as Green as Norwich, and it seems in keeping with the place's character that its big historical hero, Robert Kett, was a wealthy man who fought on the side of poor rustics, despite having no self-serving motivation to do so. I am currently living on Kett's side of the city. It's got nicer pubs than it once had but it's still the non-trendy side; the hilly side, without the artisan bakeries. People who've never bothered to meet Norwich spread all sorts of wildly inaccurate rumours about it. 'Everyone is inbred,' they say. 'It's really flat,' they say. Meanwhile, Norwich hears this and thinks, 'Have you even looked at me, or my contents?' Kett's Heights, the spot from which he and his rebel army besieged the city in 1549, on the edge of Mousehold Heath, is a terrific, towering vantage point from which to get the shape of the place: the tiered, compact layout that, unlike most cities, doesn't look bludgeoned by corporate progress. You gaze at the mass of the cathedral directly below you across the river, still dwarfing every other building around it after all these centuries, and you get a bit dizzy, thinking about what went into the building of its roof and spire, and then you remember exactly when that happened, and the rudimentary construction apparatus available at the time, and you get a hell of a lot dizzier. As I stood there, being dizzy for this exact reason, and trying to work out where Marks & Spencer was on the grid below me, a big dog ran up behind me and cough-barked and I turned to stroke it, only to realise it was a human jogger, choking. I withdrew my stroking hand, and the jogger ran off down the hill, continuing to choke, reminding me of one of the many reasons why I choose not to jog.

Can't. Stop. Buying. Books. I. Will. Almost. Certainly. Never. Get. Time. To. Read. Please. Send. Help.

One of the innumerable things I love about old books is that even negative descriptions of them sound very attractive: 'Foxing to several pages.' Brilliant! Who could possibly resist a bit of foxing?

A huge spider just crawled up my sleeve. I was amazed to find it was Carl, my guest bedroom spider, who is usually very emotionally distant.

Interesting the way physical pain becomes different as you get older. If I'd have had the wisdom tooth pain that is kicking the fuck out of me today when I was in my twenties, I'd have been a right mardy bastard. Now I'm just like, 'Ah, another bit of me that hurts. Oh well.'

Lots of small bits of inspired forward thinking go into making a residential street a nicer place to live and we take almost all of it for granted. Many many decades ago, somebody planted two lines of tulip trees along the road leading to the road where I live, and it means that in autumn walking along it feels like walking along an exquisite psychedelic tunnel. Some men drove through the psychedelic tunnel and came over to pollard my magnolia. I said I hadn't been told about it by my landlord but that sounded cool, and it was definitely OK by me. The men consulted their records and discovered it was a different magnolia that needed pollarding, at another house. I bid them farewell and good luck, feeling a sense of anticlimax.

SONGS FOR BREAKFASTS IN ROOMS WITH DOGS

My mum and dad's cat The Bridget returned today, after a five-day holiday prompted either by the unseasonably warm weather, or my mum and dad's other cat George poncing about and giving her a hard time, or some combination of the two. The Bridget – a mystery animal in innumerable ways – went for a lot of unannounced holidays in summer and autumn too, leading my mum to spend hours searching for her, at times finding her in fields well over a mile from their house, chasing rabbits, and once in a classroom at the local school. Sometimes my mum will drive as many as three villages away to collect her in the car, as you might with a naughty child, and The Bridget – who has a long, lanky figure reminiscent of the late American track and field athlete Florence Griffith Joyner – will spend the return journey with her paws eagerly up on the dashboard. This time, The Bridget crash-landed on my mum's pillow at 5 a.m., part-attired in moss. 'I think a witch flew by and dropped her from her broomstick,' said my mum.

*

When you're a house-hunter, what you soon start to realise is the language of house listings is one all of its own, off to the side of language used by real humans. Very little means what it says it means, and as houses get more expensive, and the competition to live in a nice one gets stiffer, meaning gets drained even further from it. 'Unique' can become another way of saying 'not on an estate, and not utterly identical to all of the houses around it'. 'Open plan' is stretched to describe a house that has one slightly larger than average room. Places are sold on the strange basis that it might be appealing to hardly ever be in them, with the use of the soulless phrase 'lock up and leave'. No landlord ever says 'pets welcome' even if they welcome pets. It's always 'pets by negotiation'. This description usually leads me to hypothesise about the nature of the negotiations: 'You can bring the smallest dog, but not the cockatiel. They're all wankers. That third cat of yours looks like a right mouthy prick, so he can live outside, in a tent.' Another phrase that often comes up nowadays is 'regret, no pets' which, with its mournful comma, never suggests to me that the regret is about the no-pets rule, but something else that lingers in the house; that it is a building centrally characterised by a lack of animals and a strong ambience of regret.

Before I found my current house, I met an amazing house online. The house ticked virtually all of the correct boxes and provided no red flags. I then looked at the house from the outside and it still looked very attractive. But when a few days later I was shown inside the house, it gave me a shiver up my spine. Then I went up a hidden staircase in the back of it and the shiver got colder. I would be very surprised if no animal or person had ever been ritually slaughtered there.

Yesterday a stranger outside a pub shouted, 'Get back to Woodstock!' at me. I told her that I'd been trying to for a long time but that sort of pressure doesn't help.

I queued in the local shop behind a very old lady with a tiny dog. The very old lady fumbled for coins for several minutes then, realising she didn't have quite enough, began to haggle with the cashier over the price of her shopping. The cashier explained that the price of shopping was set in stone by a vast, anonymous corporate entity and wasn't a matter for debate. Her manner was weary, suggesting this wasn't the first time the very old lady had haggled over her shopping bill. A man behind me in the queue huffed, then defected to the automated checkout. The very old lady's face was full of amazing narrative lines – deeper than the lines on most old faces – but her limbs still looked incongruously strong and I suspected she'd have been handy in a fight only two or three years ago. I looked for cash in my pocket, in case I could help her out, but I had none. She wore white, apparently brandless Velcro trainers, which had almost certainly not been purchased within the last twenty years. Her tiny dog, scarcely bigger than one of the trainers, snuffled about, looking gentle and bewildered. I stared at the dog and worried about its fragility: it looked so breakable. A whack from an angry Hobbit wielding a feather would probably hurt more than a nip from its teeth – not that it looked like it would ever even think of biting anyone. A young mother and her child arrived in the queue, while the very old lady continued to search for coins. The child approached the miniature dog, cooing. 'Don't you worry, my lovey, he won't hurt you,' said the very old lady, apparently without sarcasm.

Coffee mugs are a mystery. You get a coffee mug thinking 'this is the one', then you end up loving a coffee mug you barely initially noticed.

Two visits from neighbouring animals this morning: firstly Falcon, the hen I take care of jointly with my neighbours, to eat the wildflower seeds I've scattered, then my landlord's three-legged terrier, Cookie, for what has become her daily tummy rub. I do not think I have ever met a friendlier or more optimistic dog than Cookie, who, rather than wallowing in her disability, has turned it into a strength, powering herself around the woodland between my house and my landlord's, in the process beefing up her one front leg and giving it such a comical muscularity that I suspect she could deck the husky next door with one casual swipe. Apparently my landlord originally wanted to call her Eileen ("I lean") before the suggestion was vetoed by his partner and children.

Dogs are often lovely but I don't trust their opinions. If a cat recommended me an album it had bought, I'd totally check it out. If a dog did the same, I'd promise to listen to the album, out of politeness, but with no intention of actually doing so.

The pleasing, unexpected revelation you find after shedding a large amount of possessions is that you're still a person.

Maybe there was a time in my life, a brief long-ago point of naivete, that I fantasised about living in a big house. If so, I can't remember it. I never fantasise about living in big houses now, not even living in slightly big houses. When some people see a big house they think, 'I will live in a place like that one day, when I am rich and famous.' When I see a big house I think, 'Fucking hell, what a nightmare the cleaning and heating and maintenance must be in that place.'

My friend Phoebe is briefly lodging with me. She likes to rip open a central hole in crisp packets with her teeth, turning them into a sort of floppy dish, and leaves her muesli in a sunny spot for an hour before eating it. It's not the same way I approach muesli, by any means, but neither is it the weirdest breakfast habit I've seen. When I was fourteen, a young Portuguese golfer called Alfonso stayed at my house on an exchange trip and every morning would drink a bowl of milk with eight or nine cornflakes floating on top of it. For each day of the week he stayed, my mum made packed lunches for Alfonso and me to take out with us to the golf course. After he'd gone, she opened the window to the spare bedroom and found seven uneaten sandwiches on the ledge beyond it.

People say that moving house and divorce are the two most stressful experiences in life. This isn't true. The most stressful experience in life is trying to change a duvet cover when you've just come back from the pub and you're very tired.

I went to the auction up the road. I was more confident than I'd been at auctions in the past but still a bit worried that by accidentally blinking at the auctioneer, I might end up buying a three-thousand-pound sofa or a kitsch 1970s painting I didn't want. The auctioneer spoke very clearly, and worked the crowd. She was in the zone, and I sensed a warm-up routine, something that had happened moments before, behind a curtain. I failed to bid high enough on the chair I wanted. It went to a man with a cigarette in the furthest corner of his mouth. The room got clearer very quickly, various items being efficiently wheeled and carried out of the room by the auctioneer's colleagues. People got tired, but she stayed alert, in the zone, mixing furniture jazz speak with stand-up comedy and a touch of inadvertent poetry. 'Octagonal footstool for those with octagonal feet,' she announced. 'Disembodied hand. I've lost you.'

My parents bought their current house in 1999 and, for the first few years that they lived there, there wasn't a lot of it. Due to the limited space upstairs, when I came to stay I slept on a couple of large sofa cushions in the tiny living room, in which I felt I could sense the not unkind spirit of the house's previous owner, Dorothy House, who had died there on her hundredth birthday. Because Dorothy House had lived in the house her entire life – first with her parents, then with her husband William, who ground ball bearings for a living, and then alone – and because it had never been my childhood home, I found it a little difficult to initially perceive it as truly my parents' house. The fact that Dorothy House had the word 'House' in her name seemed to somehow underline the sense that the building was still hers.

It's interesting, when you're looking at houses to rent, that it's often the dingiest, dirtiest, most tastelessly decorated places that stipulate 'NO PETS' most violently. Have the landlords of these houses ever considered that truly discerning pets might not actually *want* to live in them?

After a lot of persuasion, the landlord of my friend Fiona's flat agreed to let her have her cat Dennis in the flat with her but said he would need references for Dennis first. A policeman friend of Fiona's agreed to be a referee. 'If Dennis was a human, I wouldn't arrest him,' the policeman wrote, ushering Dennis smoothly through the referencing process.

Overheard train chat between two hard-looking youths:
Youth one: 'I got déjà vu, man. I saw this dog and felt like I'd seen it before.'
Youth two: 'That's not déjà vu. You just saw a dog twice.'

There was a meeting at the town hall about the plans for the building next to my house to be developed into flats and the problems this might potentially cause the town. The mayor was introduced and I realised with a certain amount of surprise – but perhaps not as much surprise as some other people would have felt, in some other places – that the mayor was my postman.

Wasp.

*

Utterly unrealistic, especially in terms of financial survival in the modern age, but in an ideal world, after you'd written a book, you'd never promote it, look at it or speak about it ever again. You'd draw a firm line under it and think only about what you were doing next.

I could live without almost all of the things that come with writing, but I couldn't live without writing. If I was told I was never allowed to publish another word, I'd still have to write. Then, if you cut off my electricity, and stole all my paper and pens, I'd still find a way to carry on. I'd write short stories on a lettuce leaf with the sharpened tip of a carrot. I'd live in a cave and scratch stories on the wall by candlelight. I fear that if I didn't write, my bones would decay and soon crumble to dust. A strong notion I often get these days is that I'd like to give up writing in order to focus more seriously on my writing.

It's sweet when people tell me about some metal dangling off my car and mistake me for someone who might get that fixed within seven or eight months.

I was all packed, and unusually organised, on moving day. Then my movers didn't turn up. I got a call two hours after they were supposed to arrive to say that they'd broken down. I asked if they could come later that day. They said it was impossible. I asked if they could come the next day. They said that was impossible too. I had been told the person in charge of the company was a friendly-looking bloke called David, who asked me via email in our initial correspondence to 'give him a call any time'. You can't actually speak to David, though: the number he gives you takes you

through to a call waiting queue. In my complaint to the company, I pointed out to one of the company's managerial staff that the false intimacy of this mysterious person called David was very misleading. He explained that an email from a fake individual such as this to encourage a false sense of confidence was 'standard practice these days'. I was quite close to losing my rag at this point, but stayed relatively calm, although I did ask him a couple of questions. 'So what you're essentially saying is it's OK to be a phoney bullshitting twat these days because everybody else is a phoney bullshitting twat these days?' was one.

My boiler has broken for the fourth time in eighteen months. The landlord has provided two temporary oil-filled heaters. I mentioned it to my dad, who listed various instances of people who have burned to death via heating appliances.

*

I lack logic and am sentimental about green things, so, after my original removal men didn't turn up, and my replacement removal men had to be remotely directed to pick up my furniture, and couldn't quite fit everything in, I decided to go on a 500-mile rescue mission to retrieve several plants from inside and outside the house I had recently stopped renting. I drove down the lanes leading to the house; very mild, English lanes, reeking of cow, speaking of tractor. I felt confused about where I lived, a little like a couple of fingers or an ankle or perhaps even half a leg was still here. I unlocked the door to the house and became more aware of its smell than ever before, which, though not especially strong, had a personality, and did not at all resemble the smell of my new house. Most of the plants had been alone for a fortnight in a stiflingly hot, glassy room. Some of them had died. One was looking healthier than ever before. You never know with plants.

My dad often loses me at night. I am a few inches taller than my dad, but in his dreams I am tiny, and he is often forgetting where he put me, before locating me in coat pockets and empty coffee mugs. Sometimes in the dreams, I take the form of a bird and fly away. One night last month my mum woke to a duet: my dad shouting in his sleep and their cat The Bridget wailing. In my dad's dream on this particular night a boxer dog had me in its mouth and was running away with me, and he had grabbed its tail in an attempt to stop it. 'Fortunately The Bridget didn't seem hurt afterwards, just a bit upset,' my mum assured me.

FUTURE FUNK DYSTOPIA

In eras to come, the rise of plastic will surely be remembered as humanity's most baffling collective delusion. How did we ever not realise our use of it would kill the world? All those years, all those people, trusting that bins were some miraculous portal to a universe where man-made crap vanished. Once you're tuned into the problem, you find yourself looking at everything around you differently: Remembrance Day Poppies, clothing tags, crisp packets, the cellophane on paper bread bags that lets you see the bread, cat food pouches. It's all been said a lot recently: for change to really happen, it needs to come from corporations, from those in power, not just from the consumer habits of individuals. But that's no reason not to change your consumer habits as an individual. I'm trying my best, thinking of ways I can change, and be better, and that, by extension, is making me think about what I truly need in my life on a day-to-day basis. I don't feel I'm doing anywhere near enough. I have a metal water canister I take with me everywhere, and I've decided to totally stop buying new clothes, besides underwear, and that I probably need to give up crisps. I wish I was brave enough to give up my car. I am not doing enough and I need to try harder. I talk to people every week who are having similar revelations. But you look at the advertising around you, even sometimes the part of it that has begun to make slight ecological concessions, and you realise you're not in the majority. Capitalism is still telling people that all this convenience we've been treated to on an increasing scale for the last half century or so is not enough; that we should want more, that we 'deserve' it. Advertising tells us that it's a drag to have to still type in your PIN on payments of over £30, that high-speed rail links aren't high speed enough, that your car needs to be bigger or you're not a person, that you need a plastic window to see your bread. It's all bullshit, insidious mind control whose true purpose is to make the rich richer, not to make anyone's life simpler or happier, and whose ultimate by-product is a planet destroyed by the attendant trash of mega-convenience. The big lie that corporations flourish on is that we need more convenience, that we deserve it, whatever the cost to the planet. But why? Why *should* trains be quicker? Why *should* technology be quicker? When will this state of nirvana that it's all leading to occur, where each person will operate at peak speed and be perfectly happy and undelayed and no longer have to walk or use their mind?

It's really hard for countries not to be crap since all the people best qualified to run a country would never in a billion years want to run a country.

I phoned a stranger – elderly, was my assumption – and he picked up his phone not by saying 'Hello' but by saying the number of his phone and it felt like just about the quaintest and most genuinely old-fashioned thing you could experience in the current era. His voice sounded like a tunnel leading to a kitchen in the middle of the twentieth century.

'HE'S THE KIND OF BLOKE I WOULD HAVE ENDED UP IN A FIGHT WITH WHEN I WAS YOUNGER,' my dad says of Darren, the BBC weatherman, as we watch the TV. 'WE'D HAVE HAD A PERSONALITY CLASH. I JUST KNOW IT.'

*

I do not remember living in the eighties and the early nineties and being unaware of the existence of the Internet and mobile phones, and thinking, 'I wish somebody would hurry up and make the Internet and mobile phones happen.' I listened to music, I read books, I played sport, I walked down the jitty up to the woods, I drove over to the Peak District and had a picnic, I called friends on the phone, I caught the bus into town and met friends in the market square by the left lion at a pre-arranged time. If someone was late, you waited for them, then you went to the pub, which was one of only two pubs you ever went to, so they'd know to find you in there anyway. One time Surreal Steve, who lived rurally like me where there was a limited bus service, was really really late, and the rest of us went to a different pub to normal, which somebody said had a good Screaming Trees song on the jukebox. But even that was OK. Surreal Steve just waited for us outside the club we were going to. We found him sitting on the steps, a couple of hours later, wearing a Seal t-shirt and a bandana, and looking a bit sad. But in those days Steve had an imaginary dog who went with him almost everywhere, so at least he wasn't totally alone.

I didn't see Surreal Steve much during the last decade. When we finally caught up in Wetherspoons in Bingham, after an eight-year break, I was pleased to discover he still had his imaginary dog, which hadn't been with him last time I'd seen him. The dog was very old now, and less active, and mostly just slept under the table while we talked.

I do enjoy being alive but it's very expensive nowadays.

Given a choice, I would definitely take the old version of the Devil, who rode his wild horses through the sky onto church spires and put curses on barns, over the new one, who encourages widespread paranoia and anxiety and fucks up people's brains by designing apps for phones.

At sixteen, I had a limited sense of how big the world was, which, with the way technology has progressed, it will be impossible for a provincial sixteen-year-old to have ever again – in the same way, at least. Until everything collapses, and we all have to start again. I had thought up to that point that the people you could potentially fall in love with were limited to the people in the village where I lived, my school, which by this point I had left, and the girls who worked in the bar at the golf course I played at, who were all eighteen or nineteen, so too old for me anyway. It was exciting to start going into town and realise there were at least eight or nine more people you could potentially fall in love with.

'Weird' very rarely actually means 'weird'. A lot of the time it's just a word that boring people use to describe people with an imagination.

My friends Michelle and Sara tried to buy a loaf of bread from the all-night petrol station in Wells, the smallest city in England. The man in the kiosk wouldn't sell it to them because it wouldn't fit through the gap under the window. The bread was sliced, so Sara suggested feeding it through the gap, piece by piece, which would absolutely have worked, but the man refused, on the basis that he wasn't authorised to do that.

The foliage has died back, revealing the roads leading to the motorway to be herbaceous borders of litter. Not even the blood and bone we left on our battlefields did any damage. Quite the opposite. Our suffering enriched the planet. Now our long, easy, lazy, convenient lives kill it.

The year's days are at their darkest. I've paid my chiropractor bill, and my tax bill, and my rent, and the bill for the new brakes on my car, and the other stuff they found wrong with my car when they fixed the brakes. I have a chest infection and I have lost my favourite jumper. Life isn't always easy. While campaigning for his fourth term as prime minister, in his eighties,

William Gladstone was struck violently in the eye by a piece of gingerbread and attacked by a mad cow. During certain periods of history, you could be sewn inside a camel for not believing in a god nobody had even talked about a couple of centuries earlier. In the 1200s the Bishop of Exeter was beheaded with a bread knife. When Eleanor Roosevelt stayed at Buckingham Palace and a servant ran a bath for her, she was shocked and upset by how shallow the water was.

The harsh truth of adulthood: time flies when you're not having fun as well.

I look back fondly on an era when 'utterly overwhelmed by everything all the time' wasn't the standard human mind state.

One great and underrated thing about winter is when a cat with cold fur returns to the house from the great outdoors, demands to be stroked and tells you about all the banal nonsense it's been up to.

February: the unnecessary encore winter does to please its hardcore fans.

One winter a legendary amount of snow fell and school was closed and the phone lines in the village came down, but when we picked up the phone at our house there were sometimes strangers instantly there on the line. During the same epoch in British history adverts were broadcast during the intermissions in films and sports coverage that I stayed up late to watch, which told you about phone lines where you could chat to strangers, just about stuff, nothing obviously salacious. In the adverts the strangers always seemed to be happy and having parties with balloons and fizzy drinks, and would let you join in, we were told, for a fixed rate of pence per minute. But the strangers who were on the phone when I picked it up after the snow didn't charge you a fixed rate of pence per minute to speak to them; you didn't even have to dial a number to get through to these strangers, and you could talk to them for free. One day after school, before my mum and dad were home from work, I picked up the phone and two girls were on the other end of the line. They said they were a year older than me and from Bulwell, seven miles east of where I lived, which at the time seemed far away without being at all exotic. I talked to the girls for around an hour and they teased me with questions that seemed advanced, even next to some of the stuff I had heard discussed by the girls in my year at school, who I have since realised were quite advanced themselves in the grander context of late twentieth-century adolescent sexual knowledge countrywide. The girl whose phone it was asked me if I had any nice friends because the boys in Bulwell were all shit and I said I did and she gave me her number. I told Lee about it the next day at school and he seemed excited too, even though he hadn't met the girls and had no idea what they looked like and I had passed on minimal information about their hobbies and personalities, so I gave him the girl's number, and both of us were on a bit of a high about it for the rest of the day, but neither of us ever did call the number. The following week in biology I noticed that someone had scratched it into the desk with a pen, quite deep.

One winter I mistimed an afternoon walk and completed the last two miles of it after the sun had vanished beneath the long edge of the land. My route took me past a Bronze Age burial mound which gave me an idea for a novel that I was not yet capable of writing.

One winter I fell asleep on top of a hot water bottle, and it seriously burned my leg. The burn turned into an unsightly, furious blister and left a large scar, still clearly visible today when I am trouserless, which hints at a far more heroic backstory.

One winter I walked with Will and Mary past Ice Age pond-swamps and hairy cows that watched us dolefully from dark woods and we cracked the natural frosted glass skin on puddles with our heels and at the end of the walk we all admired the way the sun looked against the low white-red sky, then realised it was actually the moon, not the sun.

One winter – well, actually it was spring, but it was a cold day, and felt like spring experiencing accelerated nostalgia for winter – I walked back from the pub with Pat and Rachel, and Pat told us to look at the moon, which was shining amazingly brightly through the trees, and Rachel and I waited a minute or two before explaining to Pat that it was actually a streetlight, not the moon.

'YOU KNOW WHAT I LEARNED TODAY?' my dad asks. 'What's that?' I reply. 'HOW TO LOOK AT ALL THE PHOTOS I'VE TAKEN ON MY PHONE,' he says. 'I'D NEVER SEEN THEM.'

I prefer January to December but I perceive its many drawbacks, particularly for the self-employed. In the dark tiny days, just as you're starting to forget spring can ever be a thing again, you remember it's time to pay your tax. In my case, that brings a concomitant reality check, and a release from any financial delusions I might have been harbouring in the preceding months. Another year has gone by and I have not earned more than the previous year, not earned nearly as much as I was earning early in my adulthood, not nearly as much as most proper people of my age. Another book has been written but nothing has changed, financially speaking. Can I do anything to alter that? I doubt it. And anything I might strive to do would certainly be damaging to my work. Time to step back, get real, recommit to dying penniless. It's freeing, once you look it square in the face. Then the motivation comes flooding in: to write, to improve, to learn, to explore, to enjoy what I have.

I have been lucky enough to know true love in my life. There was also the time the actor Damian Lewis winked at me and said, 'Nice shirt.'

Loads of people start sentences with 'So...' at the moment. It's been happening very noticeably for about three years. I imagine it's probably something to do with diminished attention spans, and the fact that 'So...' is quite a good way to get people's attention and convey a sense that you're about to make an involving and well-explained statement. I'm sure I've slipped into the habit on occasion, and I've had a word with myself about it. Some people who don't start sentences with 'So...' have been a bit mean about people who start sentences with 'So...', but there are definitely worse things a person can do than start a sentence with 'So...'

The way we're structuring and growing the world is cramping freedom but also making more people seduced by freedom's possibilities which makes freedom even more cramped.

You don't need music at swimming pools, but I'm not talking about it to strangers anymore. The last time I talked about not needing music at swimming pools to a stranger, the stranger then proceeded to corner me in the hot tub at the pool where I swim and list his other complaints about modern life, which included men who look like women, women who look like men, and all the environmentalists you get these days, who won't let you eat a sausage anymore. As the man moved up through his gearbox of outrage, covering such other subjects as Why It's a Shame There Are No Longer Any Comedians Like Benny Hill, I glanced out of the corner of one eye towards the steps leading from the hot tub to freedom and listened for a tiny gap in his monologue, looking for my escape route. What was perhaps even more disturbing than the man's opinions was his assumption that I, someone he had just met, would naturally share them. He began to tell me about his personal regrets in life, as well his regrets about what all of life had become for everyone in the twenty-first century, and, even though he was only six years older than me, I felt like I was talking to someone from another epoch, an actual fossil; one that you might find pressed into a remaining section of wall from a terrible nightclub that got bulldozed in 1988 to make way for a health centre. I go to the swimming pool to swim, not for any ancillary lifestyle aspects the pool attempts to provide, and my gut instinct in the past had always told me to avoid the hot tub, that the hot tub might be a place where something excruciating could well happen to me, and the experience confirmed, as so many of my experiences do, that a gut instinct is usually correct. Now, once again, I steer well clear of the tub, just as I steer well clear of the music the pool plays, by hiding from it underwater. My dad has also lost patience with the music being played at his local swimming pool, and recently taped cardboard over the speakers in the changing room, but he said the tape he brought wasn't strong enough, and the cardboard soon fell off. I don't even know where the speakers are at my local pool, which is a bigger complex than my dad's local pool, with an army of bored-looking employees and far more rules, so I wouldn't bother trying to do the same thing. Instead, I just try to hold my breath through Coldplay and Ed Sheeran and that awful Sting song where he sings about New York and that awful Black Eyed Peas song about a good night which you know, instinctively, when you hear it, must have actually been a hideous night. When the aqua aerobics class takes over, I simmer with quiet envy, wondering why they get the ebullience of the Bee Gees and Chic and Donna Summer and we don't. Are swimmers not allowed to be happy? All the pool music played when aqua aerobics isn't taking place comes across as joyless soundvertising: songs written not because they need to be written, but cynically constructed with the anodyne mood of a high-street clothes shop or a multinational leisure complex in mind. I carry on doing lengths, and fantasise about spring, when I will be back in the sea, and the soundtrack will be only the waves, the shifting stones, the weather and the countless life forms going about their business under the surface.

I wonder if the first truck driver to have the idea of overtaking another truck driver really slowly on a motorway had any idea of the potential knock-on effect of his actions in the wider scheme of things and how many people he would eventually make unhappy.

Nobody thinks they're part of history as it's happening. Nobody who isn't a massive bighead, anyway.

A thing I especially love about animals is they never part-read pieces of writing online then screenshot out-of-context segments from them.

One of many excellent aspects of bats is that they rarely go on social networking apps and rant and condemn other bats in a way that suggests they have no grasp of nuance and wish to remake the world entirely in their own image.

*

Wolves have done some bad stuff but to their credit they almost never post photos of other wolves looking undignified on public transport.

There was a point in my life where I thought the world was evolving in a way where people would gradually talk less shit but it turns out I was wrong. Somewhere history took another turn, and to speak in sentences made up entirely of bubbles of rancid hot air became the norm. 'Influencer', 'reaching out', 'networking' – these are now phrases people use with either no awareness of how grasping and unpleasant it makes them sound, or total awareness of that coupled with a hard-faced chutzpah about it. I will never reach out, I am not interested in influencing anybody to do anything other than maybe casually check out a record or book I've enjoyed or be nicer to animals and the environment, and if some networking is happening I will go to a quiet place where it is not happening and hide. I don't have a network. I have some mates. My network is an old broken cobweb in my bathroom that I'm trying to rescue a moth from.

I suppose I am guilty, like many people who have spent most of their life living in rural areas a long way from the capital, of not viewing it as a real place, or at least viewing it as a place coated in too much man-made hardness and fear to give rise to any comforting huddles of real community. In a small bit of free time between talks and catching up with friends I wandered around the fringes of Camden and Hampstead, thinking about the London underneath the London I could see, wondering how you teased it out, and marvelling at the confidence with which the houses, for centuries, had been built; grand important buildings for grand important people. I popped

68

into the post office on Haverstock Hill and got told off for queuing from the wrong side, as did a man called Albert, who was after me in line. Albert laughed about this, speaking to me as you might a fellow naughty lad at your school, and told me he was ninety-two. I said he didn't look ninety-two. He said his secret was an apple a day. He then told me he'd been in Sudan during the war, then worked in the London sewers for six years, before becoming the archivist for Hampstead, and still talked about the place as if it was, say, a village in Worcestershire. I wanted to know his life story, but at this point the woman behind the counter barked at me to get in front of her and get on with my transaction.

Email from my dad. No subject heading. Just says 'WE ARE LIVING IN THE AGE OF THE GIT.' Nothing else. His pillow is still at my house, he tells me later that day. He stayed here six nights ago and has only just noticed.

I bumped into my old friend in the Co-op, where he was buying wine. He invited me back to his place, where we drank the wine and he told me about a hexagonal gemstone he'd found while dowsing a dew pond in the area. He then got some plastic boxes out with numbers on and made a tower out of them in his kitchen and told me that he'd worked out that the year 2026 was when it was all going to end, or at least when it was going to start again, in some new way. Even though he lost me a little as he explained why, it made me think about a lot of stuff. What it mostly made me think is that I didn't have much time left to read all the books I wanted to.

WEATHER-FUCKED PELT OF A
LONG-DECEASED VOLE

I walked to the heath. The first time I had walked to the heath was ten years ago, to play pitch and putt with my friends Jamie and Russ. I don't remember who won but I remember that Jamie and Russ looked immaculate, as they always do, and we saw a young woman successfully meeting the conflicting needs of three ferrets on leads. Just beyond the border on the other side of the heath is a shock of farmhouse, with a tree house, arched windows and lots of unused outdoor space. It's a very fenland, not very Norwich building: a piece of the stark, utilitarian countryside incongruously sprawled in a leafy corner of city, as if injured after falling out the back of a vast truck. As I passed it now, my path crossed that of a man in a leather waistcoat with big bare arms, a ponytail and thin black trousers like the ones I was told I had to wear when I worked in a chain pub, where, a lot like the American-themed Zaks Diner – which dominates the centre of the heath – cold baked beans eaten by children with tiny forks smeared the tables, and left me for several years afterwards with a disliking for baked beans and an aversion to tiny forks. It was January when I walked past the man and a wind from the North Sea had hacked and chiselled its way into my bones. A terrier stood and appeared to think deep existential thoughts in a gigantic nearby puddle, all but a centimetre or two of its legs covered by the cold, wind-swirled water. I walked on, up to Catton Park and the beautiful church behind it, in the old village, near the cat and barrel village sign. The sign was erected in 1936 to commemorate the coronation of King George VI, but the symbolism goes back to Tudor times, when Old Catton was known for its population of wild cats. During the mid-twentieth century, the sign was stolen several times, but always retrieved, once from nearby farmland and once from Stockton-on-Tees, 224 miles away.

*

The heath once stretched much further. My house, if it had existed then, would have been part of it. Now it's on a road of ex-local authority buildings. Nearly all of them are big and solid with matching red-brown brick, and have very green spacious gardens, reminding you that there was once a time that people in positions of authority did not think poor people should have to live in horrible places. All my neighbours seem to have been here forever. Allie and John next door arrived in 1963. Pam, at the top of the road, moved in during the summer of 1974. In the evening I sometimes see Allie and John walking down to the meadow by the river, hand in hand.

I used to think people who said, 'I wouldn't live in Norfolk because of the water' were silly. I don't now. In Norfolk, I yearn for the delicious, soft water of west Devon, and the slightly less delicious and soft water of east Somerset. The water is so hard in Norfolk it's pretty much aroused. What it does to your kettle and your hot drinks is bad; what it does to your hair is worse. After just one hair wash in Norfolk it feels like what I have on my head is not hair at all but the downtrodden weather-fucked pelt of a long-deceased vole.

Most bottled water tastes nothing like water. Volvic is in fact 96% steel. Then there's Evian, which tastes like milk from an awful cottage.

Rosie and I went to the other side of the city to see some gardens. We talked about nominative determinism, which is one of Rosie's favourite subjects, to the extent that she has come up with the opposing concept of 'nominative negativism', to describe a situation where a person develops characteristics that are the antithesis of what their name suggests. The gardens seemed an apt place for the topic of nominative determinism, as it appeared to happen frequently to the horticulturally inclined. Bob Flowerdew, Alan Bloom and Rose Dejardin all grew up to be very successful gardeners. Another man called Alan let us into the gardens, even though we only had £3.81 in change, and it was cash only and the actual price was £4. He told us not to tell Brian, who was over near the cakes, so we didn't.

In the cemetery, there were rabbits and a lone, pale ginger-haired boy and I noticed a cloth cap had been left hanging on one of the graves. The cemetery is wild and beautiful and was built to provide a new, non-denominational space in 1821, when the other cemeteries in the city were overflowing with corpses to the extent that body parts were often pushed back above the surface. People worried that the overcrowding was affecting the water supply, since most parish pumps were located next to cemeteries. The water from one Norwich pump was described as 'almost pure essence of churchyard'. I moan about the water in modern Norfolk but I have found myself doing so less since regularly walking through the cemetery.

For centuries, strange beasts have been spotted in the waves, at the eastern extremities of Suffolk and Norfolk: giant serpents, a sermonising beflippered clergyman. I want to believe all of them exist, but on a wild day at Horsey Gap, when the sea mist is up and a seal pops its head up from the surf twenty yards ahead of me, I can – especially if I squint a bit – understand a more rational explanation. There are few better places in Britain in November than Horsey to witness the habits of grey seals or, as they were sometimes referred to in the 1500s by those with an overactive ecclesiastical imagination, 'sea bishops'. Right now, there are dozens of them on the beach, mating and giving birth and yawning and stretching like lovely, big, old velvet post-prandial aquatic professors. The advisory signs and volunteer seal wardens at Horsey rightly advise not to go within ten metres of the seals, which, fortunately, is easily close enough to see the sad, beautiful intelligence in their eyes and begin to understand the more-eclectic-than-you-thought nature of seal life; all the different dappled shapes and all the soft and gruff and light and heavy character within it. The car park costs three pounds, none of which, scandalously, goes to seals, so I would advise leaving your car further away – perhaps doing a picturesque, reed-heavy walk from Horsey Windpump, which, if you manage not to immediately begin repurposing it as an insult to describe various prominent Tory politicians, you're a more restrained person than me. This walk will take you past the Brograve drainage mill, which, not long after its construction in the mid-1700s, the Devil tried and failed to blow down. Inaccessible from the footpath, but viewable from the other side of Waxham's new-cut drainage ditch, the latter mill is now a slightly leaning wreck inhabited by cormorants, greylag geese and ghosts. As I watched a cormorant balance on its sail, like some omen of Broadland death, I listened for the wailing of drowned children, which is said to be heard coming from Horsey Mere on quiet, cold days. The wailing of the ghost children would not be quite in close enough proximity to harmonise with the sound of the seals on the beach, who can be quite noisy; an attribute that makes one of the collective nouns for seals, 'rookery', a tiny bit less confusing. Horribly, several seals have recently been seriously injured by plastic objects at Horsey. As I thought about this and watched a mother seal visibly panic as a passing couple let their dog get too close to her and her pup, I fantasised about a world where humans and their indulgences did not impact on these magnificent creatures, and I did not mourn our absence.

'Yes! Let's not drink,' says one of the two men on the table adjacent to me in the pub, taking a long sip of his beer. 'Let's do stuff.'

*

On New Year's Day I walked at Hardley Flood, not realising that there was another flood, as well as the permanent official Flood on the map, and the footpath was closed. In hindsight, I did think the bit where I had to climb through a tree, then negotiate my way across a deep inlet of the river along a thin plank and an even thinner plank, both slick and slimy with a substance not unlike tar, seemed a little extreme. Only when I got back to the village newsagent and saw the headline about the nearby pub currently only accessible by boat did it all start to make sense. Out beyond the Flood, the other flood had lifted old litter from the river, spreading it evenly among the water-flattened reeds, uncovering an uncomfortable truth. I'd been moaning a bit a few days before about the tameness of the Norfolk countryside, but the stretch of ground beyond the water got wilder and wilder, and I felt it would just continue to get wilder after that, forever, with no return to civilisation, which some might actually argue to be the truth, depending on how they feel about Great Yarmouth, which could be found a few miles on in the same direction. I saw a little egret and a big bouncing hare, then beyond that, on the lane, a stray hubcap and red berries that pierced the sombre light and a fat squashed rat in its last stage of ratness before merging forever with the mud. Heavy footsteps thundered towards me out of nowhere from the rear as dusk fell, and I turned, bracing myself for the running stranger who would plough into me, knock me flat to the ground and rob me, only to realise what I'd heard was the strong, sure, portentous wingbeat of a swan, cruising only four or five feet over my head.

I thought I saw a wheelbarrow in the middle of the road leading down towards the city from my house but it was a man doing press-ups.

A scarecrow has been stolen from the village of Wighton. Residents are very upset. In Barsham, just over the border into Suffolk, I pass the giant biscuit-headed tree scarecrow, built during the 1970s by the organisers of the old Barsham Faire, which resembles a monster from a futuristic lo-fi horror film, and makes me think how few good scarecrows I've seen in Norfolk and Suffolk recently.

Norwich is a quiet and mild city, although I perhaps didn't realise how quiet and mild until I walked through it with my dad, who is neither of these things. My mum and I kept losing my dad, then realising he had stopped to take a photo of some people sitting on a bench who he thought looked interesting, or to pretend to shout abuse at someone on a loud motorbike, or to try to sneak onto the end of a guided history tour and consume some of the information for free. 'LOOK AT THIS, IT'S FUCKING AMAZING!' my dad said, as we reached Pulls Ferry, the fifteenth-century flint watergate near the cathedral. 'WHY HAVE YOU NEVER SHOWN ME IT BEFORE?' 'I showed you it in 2005 and 2009,' I said. 'NO YOU DIDN'T,' said my dad. 'I'D KNOW IF YOU HAD.' I noticed that nobody else in Norwich was as loud as my dad, or as keen to make friends with strangers. I began to feel like someone leading a large, inquisitive dog through a lawn bowls event, with a blaring radio attached to the dog's collar. 'I am charmed by this dog's enthusiasm but why don't its owners turn the radio down?' I imagined the bowls players thinking. But what the bowls players didn't realise was that the radio didn't have a volume switch, just one marked 'ON' and another marked 'OFF', and that these switches controlled the dog too, not just the radio.

Message from my mum: 'I'm waking up with an itchy nose and swollen eyes every morning. I think I have to stop the cat sleeping on my face.'

A thing I will remember, when I'm gone from the city, which, in truth, was always going to be quite soon after I arrived here, because I am not a City Person, is how rattled I was by the sirens. So many of them. 'Who is dying?' I would find myself thinking. 'Which significant building are we in danger of losing through fire?' It was like being slapped around the face by my bumpkinhood. Constant sirens and ice cream vans: that was my garden soundtrack for my first months here. The song of crime, interspersed with the song of sugar. On a walk around the northern part of the city, I found the cul-de-sac where the ice cream vans sleep at night. Three of them, anyway. I am not sure if the vans all belonged to the same person or if it was just a road that the kind of people who own ice cream vans tended to be drawn to as a place to live. I have heard it can be a very competitive trade. My friend Adi attempted to get a career as an ice cream man off the ground a few years back but was bullied off whichever patch he tried to set up on by more established rivals. Perhaps these territorial wars were why the ice cream vans played their songs so loud, and so often.

*

Yet, simultaneously, the silence often stuns me, here on the green fringe. It's quiet in an entirely different way to the very rural house I moved from, where agricultural machinery and speeding cars cut sharply through a bigger emptiness. At night, the silence is thick, but a few sounds still slice it up, all of them haunting and not typically urban. The honk of trains is a ghostly wail circling the house which seems to come from no place where there is a track and continues far beyond the parameters of National Rail timetables. Meanwhile, in the woods up the hill, on the edge of something created by the night, muntjac deer gather in groups and bark incantations into the early hours. It makes the foliage seem deeper than it is and the proximity of Aldi and Nails By Nonie and senior lettings negotiators and Halfords seem impossible. A hedgehog snuffled about outside my bedroom for several nights, creating a noise twice the size of itself, then eventually – on hot evenings when I left the back door ajar – began letting itself in and helping itself to my cats' food. The hedgehog's attitude to me became gradually more nonchalant, and by a certain point it would not have surprised me in the slightest to find him stretched out upside down on my bed, paws splayed, greeting me with a casual yawn as I rummaged for my pyjama bottoms. I arrived home from the pub one night with my friend Louise and, as I boiled the kettle, noticed the hedgehog napping in the corner, beneath the cutlery drawer. Louise continued the anecdote she was telling me, without missing a beat, as, listening, I returned the hedgehog to its natural environment. 'Was I so drunk last night that I thought it was perfectly normal for you to gently pick a sleeping hedgehog up from your kitchen floor and take it outside?' Louise asked the next day. 'Yes,' I answered. 'You were.'

THE TROUBLE WITH SHEDS

Swimming in thick warm rain. A pungent, seaweedy cove. Goat-like sheep on the cliffs above me. One or two walkers, but nobody else. A rope on the steep cliff path to help me back up. The rain is different in Devon to many other, flatter places because you're often in the cloud. I like being in the cloud. Sometimes you're still in the cloud, even on the beach. On days like this you just crave the rain and the salt of the sea and the wind on you, like other people crave chocolate or shoes or heroin.

Where is this place that is the centre of everywhere, that people are referring to, when they say stuff is 'far away'? I don't think it's London, although London obviously has an influence on those conversations. People often say, 'Ooh, that's FAR' when I tell them I live in Devon. But that is just an opinion. Devon isn't far from Devon.

*

I walked the Glastonbury site a week after the festival's final curtain. It seemed even more vast than it did when it was full of people: a post-apocalyptic dust city, overrun with gulls. Dead badgers ringed its tarmac borders. I'm one of those unusual Outdoor People who is also Not Really a Festival Person, and I'd had misgivings about agreeing to talk on stage at the festival, having discovered its founder, Michael Eavis, was a supporter of the badger cull. Three days before the start of the festival, on a lane over two miles from the festival gates, my car was flagged down by an aggressive security guard, who, very reluctant to believe I lived nearby, told my friend Will and me about the serious terrorist threat faced by this year's festival, and instructed us, 'Believe me, you don't want to see *my* face again, so I wouldn't drive up here again in the next week, if I were you.' For someone who claimed not to want us to be on this bit of road, she seemed inordinately keen to keep us on it for as long as possible, and, after the fifth or sixth sentence she'd begun with 'I'm not being funny but...' – the central hallmark of all people who are, in fact, being funny – it became clear that, for her, this was for the most part not about security, it was about pleasure: that particular kind taken when revelling in a small amount of power. In winter, I'd walked over the edge of the festival site, not realising that was where I was, and not seen another soul. Deer leapt out of long grass, shocked out of sleep by my incongruous presence. To see the area transformed into a temporary metropolis, so quickly, was dizzying and frightening. I stood on top of the southern hill on the Friday of the festival, looking at all those lights on the opposite side of the valley, as far away as a suburb is from a humming marketplace, yet still part of this same vast gathering we were attending. It made me think of the way real cities have been made, the way they bludgeon and transform the land, and what will be found beneath them when they have rotted away.

'I HAVEN'T GOT A FORESKIN,' shouts the teenager to his friend as he pisses into my hedge, piercing everything great the morning has offered.

An old man at the swimming pool with a strong Somerset accent was talking to another man with a slightly less strong Somerset accent and saying 'Like you say...' a lot. West Country people often start a sentence with 'Like you say...' It makes you assume they are referencing something you've said, when usually they aren't at all – they could be talking about the specifics of the fire alarm drill at their workplace or Yeovil Football Club or any number of other topics you've never even discussed – but there's nothing wrong with that: it's friendly and inclusive and nice. When I first began to visit Devon a lot and met my then-girlfriend's dad, he spoke very quickly, and when talking to me started quite a few sentences with 'Like you say...' but because he spoke at such a high speed, it was only later that I had time to analyse our conversation. 'But I didn't say any of that!' I would think.

Some people in Devon say 'You're making a mountain out of a molehill' but some prefer to put it a different way, and say 'You're taking farting for sneezing'.

I walked down soft lanes past the cars of my youth, abandoned in orchards and grassy driveways, to the house of the writer Ronald Blythe. It was a very old house, and Ronald's coffee was head-meltingly strong. He didn't look eighty-seven, which is what he was. He said he had walked almost everywhere his entire life, and he lamented the way that people all make themselves 'unhealthy' and 'fat' nowadays by buying too much food from the same shops. 'People had much sharper features back when they worked in the fields,' he told me. The house belonged to the painter John Nash before Ronald, and being enclosed by its bendy old structure felt a bit like being inside a piece of subtly distorted art. The valley where it nestles is in the heart of witchfinder country and Ronald talked about the 'horribly sexual' Matthew Hopkins, self-appointed Witchfinder General of the mid-1600s, as if he was, say, someone Ronald's cousin had gone to school with, and his reign of terror had taken place just a few months ago.

A man was ahead of me in the supermarket today, buying only two items: a miniature brandy and a pork pie. 'Clive, *do not* fuck off down the wine aisle!' said a woman to another man, a few yards away.

Dorset is the county that has my favourite village names but Norfolk and Suffolk definitely have some of my favourite country signs, and lane names. On a walk on the Marriott's Way I was pleased to see the multinational horse manure sign near Reepham still going strong – if a little faded – a decade after I last saw it. Upper Goat Lane and Lower Goat Lane have always been my top two Norwich lanes, with the vivid images they conjure up of an important forgotten urban goat hierarchy, although neither have the notoriety of Sluts Hole Lane in the south Norfolk village of Besthorpe. I also like the evocative, recurring Flowerpot Lanes and Brick Kiln Lanes in and around the villages between Diss and Norwich, Big Back Lane and Trumpery Lane (discovered on explorations of the southern edge of the Broads), Pudding Bowl Lane in Reepham, Rampant Horse Street in Norwich, Blind Lane (leading to Chimney Street) and Cuckstool Lane in Castle Acre, and Judas Lane, which can be found in the Suffolk village of Mellis, not far from the moated farmhouse where the nature writer Roger Deakin lived. I can't find an official etymological explanation for the latter but I like to think it was once the address of a known local betrayer. 'I'm going down Judas Lane,' a village wag might have said once, and before you knew it, it had caught on throughout Mellis and the neighbouring villages. All this got me thinking of Ralph's Wife's Lane in the Lancashire village of Banks, named for the ghost wife of a drowned fisherman named Ralph who still wanders the lane searching for him, and in turn this put me in mind for the first time in years of a dishevelled woman who during the mid-nineties used to repeatedly walk up and down Porchester Road in Gedling in Nottingham, allegedly looking for her husband, who'd been killed on the road in a car crash several years previously. I don't know who she was or whether she's still doing her route but I would like to think that one day someone might see fit to rename the road in her honour.

You'd think garden centres might be a celebration of life but vast parts of the ones near me are devoted to death: aisles and aisles of weedkillers and pesticides. Then there's the gravel. So much gravel, of every different grade and shade any gravel enthusiast could possibly wish for. We have become a nation obsessed with gravel. It's so prevalent that seeing a green driveway feels utterly evocative, an anachronistic shock. I love these unkempt emerald carports, the sprinkle of wildflowers you often find on them in spring, the way the grass will make its creeping escape from them and lick up the side of a nearby building.

Of all the wildlife around the loveliest house I have ever lived in, what I possibly miss most is the woodpecker who used to rap on the oak tree behind my garden with his beak. Winter was hard, as it is everywhere, but that rapping began to sound like a drum roll for spring: a heralding of happy times ahead.

*

The way I view East Anglia from the West Country, at my most optimistic: an easy and effortless place, where everything is close, small, convenient and socially well-knitted. The way I view the West Country from East Anglia, at my most optimistic: a magic water and hill kingdom. The only place where I can fully be me.

My parents are in Devon, staying at my house. I'm at their house, in Nottinghamshire. My mum calls to ask me how everything is. I tell her it's fine. She's in the car, which is being driven by my dad. 'LET ME TALK TO HIM. I'VE GOT SOMETHING URGENT TO SAY,' says my dad, in the background. 'Hi,' I say. 'I JUST SAW A MAN SELLING CAULIFLOWER IN A FIELD,' says my dad.

Sheringham. I parked in the woods on the hill, almost a proper hill, even by normal topographic standards, not just Norfolk standards, and walked down through the woods towards the town. There was a carved Saxon face on a plinth in the woods and the town smelled strongly of meat. Last time I came here, in late 2013, I'd only been a vegetarian for eighteen months, and even then with a sizeable lapse in the middle of that period, so the smell of meat wasn't odd to me, but now, after seven meatless years, it was. A whole pig was roasting on the pavement and a couple of the larger dogs who were around attempted to steer their owners towards it. ANGER AT SWIMMING POOL PRICE INCREASE, said the local newspaper headline. Lots of stuff rattled and whistled. The town, every time I've been, has been enormously rattly and whistly, and it's perhaps no coincidence that many of its most famous ghosts are known for making high-pitched sounds: most notably, a drowned sailor on the part of the beach near the old bit of town, and a shrieking woman who appears whenever there is disaster on the horizon. The only rattlier, whistlier town I can think of is Teignmouth, in Devon, whose estuary bridge whistles and rattles so much in high winds, its eerie lament can be heard over a mile away. In fact, Sheringham seemed rattlier and whistlier in a much spookier way the last time I'd visited, all empty streets and portentous seagulls and old pub signs creaking in the wind, but away from the provincial clickbait and bantering butchers of its high street, the mood was taken down a notch by a scarecrow I passed in a garden on a side street: a slumped man on a garden chair, with rotting branch prongs for fingers, his face hidden inside the folds of a coat and hat blasted by so many years of weather, they'd become the actual colour of weather, or at least the colour of the kind of weather you often got in winter here: dirty, brown, eroded by salt and sea spit. No other counties do scarecrows quite like Norfolk and Suffolk. But it's never the overdone kind you get at village scarecrow festivals that linger longest in my mind after my walks here, always this more rudimentary kind, with their strong aura of death. I crept up to the fence to get a closer look, waiting for two eyes to appear at a window of the grey house the scarecrow belonged to. I walked on, to Beeston Bump, a cliff towering to a very un-East Anglian 207 feet in height, which is thought to be a lair of Black Shuck, the East Anglian Demon Dog who, in slightly different incarnations, also maintains homes in Suffolk, Essex and Cambridgeshire. In the early part of the twentieth century, the writer and folklorist W. H. Barrett met an elderly man in a pub a couple of miles west of here, at Salthouse, who claimed to have been chased home from Cromer, past Beeston Bump, by Black Shuck, back at a time when the man was first beginning to make a living by digging up lugworms and selling them as bait. When the lugworm seller reached home, he had lost his shoes. Shuck sat outside the house, waiting for him to re-emerge. His dad shot the dog several times, but each bullet passed right through its body. Later, I would think about the scarecrow a lot. There was absolutely nothing about it to suggest it was not some unloved granddad who had fallen asleep in the garden some time in 1986 and never woken up.

'I'VE JUST DONE SOMETHING REALLY SATISFYING,' my dad told me. 'What's that?' I asked. 'PULLED DOWN MY TROUSERS IN FRONT OF THE TV AND RUBBED MY BOTTOM ON *AUTUMNWATCH*.'

Old clothes are scary. I don't just mean quite old clothes. If that were true, I'd not be able to sleep in my own bedroom without the light on. I mean really old clothes: clothes full of retroactive grime and forgotten weather. After rewatching *Whistle and I'll Come to You*, the original 1968 BBC adaptation of the M. R. James story, in which Michael Hordern, the voice of Paddington, is chased by a filthy-looking rag the height of a man along a desolate beach, my girlfriend and I walked to Walberswick, in Suffolk, from Blythburgh Church. On walks, I'm always passing lost gloves and hats and mittens stuck on gateposts and stiles. Sometimes, I send photos of them to my friend Becky, and she sends one back that she's passed on a walk in Derbyshire, or Yorkshire, or Wales. Perhaps each one of these bits of knitwear contains a lost part of a person's life, but the part is very, very small, because most of the knitwear is quite new, and quite small. But sometimes there's something bigger and darker and older that you see abandoned in the countryside, and maybe it contains something more frightening. We crossed the common, where the author Penelope Fitzgerald claimed to have spotted Black Shuck late during the last century. In her telling, Shuck – or 'Chuff', or 'Old Scarf', as he is sometimes called around here – was white. We turned inland along the estuary, where boat parts clanged. The wind drained away after that, but so did the flicker of spring we'd felt in the air earlier, and we were alone in total darkness for the last mile and a half, just us and Scarf, with the silhouette of the church to guide us. At the car I took my walking boots off my squelchy feet, regarded the three big holes in them, and wondered if they'd last one more walk, just as I had for the previous twenty-three or twenty-four walks I'd taken them on. They looked far older than they were, owing to all the hammer I'd given them over these last three years, in Norfolk, and Suffolk, and Devon, and Derbyshire, and Cornwall, and Wales, and Herefordshire, and Somerset, and Worcestershire, and Dorset, and Gloucestershire, and Wiltshire, and Notts. A different colour to the one they'd been marketed as. They looked haunted, like they carried a story for each eyelet. Beside the church, the spooky angel on the village sign stretched out its wings under a single star twinkling in a clear sky. It was dark enough to believe stuff, looking at that angel. The dark made the land old again. It re-energised it as a place of conjurings and stories.

I've often wished to be able to properly communicate with my cats. I like to think about all the stuff I'd want to ask them: what sort of music they enjoy, for instance, whether they are intermittently nice to me because I give them food or because they actually like my personality, or where they sometimes sod off to at night. But I think if I was given the opportunity to say only one sentence to them in a language they'd understand, all that would quickly go out of the window. What I'd probably say to them would be: 'If you're going to puke, please do so on a hard surface.'

I'd been at my house a couple of years and there were still two or three footpaths a couple of miles away that I had never explored, so I walked the footpaths, even though they didn't go anywhere in particular. On the way back I came down a very narrow lane towards the edge of the village and saw a squashed adder, stretched out to very nearly the width of the lane. The adder had probably been minding its own business, just like most of the UK's adders who, despite their reputation for poison and venom, have not actually got it together to kill a person on this land mass since 1975.

I walked to Porlock, on the north coast. Stories in my head, my feet writing them. Stories I couldn't write if I stayed still. Deep in the woods above the waves: the tiny Culbone Church. A freshly dug mound of earth on the west side. Two local rival families are buried here, their graves facing one another. A cow once wandered into the church and pulled the bell and everyone who could hear it wondered who had died, which wasn't many people, due to the lack of houses around.

In 1750 nearly all residents of Somerset lived within ten miles of a clockmaker.

I hiked fourteen miles to find the source of the river on the moor. When I got there, I was hot and bothered, and it was just a bubble in the ground, as I'd expected it to be. The tussocks on this bit of the moor were tall and hard and there was no footpath and after a while it made me feel like the tussocks were sentient and intent on my downfall. I was ragged and dopey when I got home and hoped to rest my muscles in a hot bath but within less than a minute of my arrival one of my cats brought a screaming rabbit into the house. I prised the rabbit, miraculously unhurt, from his jaws, dropped it gently under my garden hedge, and put the kettle on, but within a minute heard the rabbit tapping on the window, asking to be let back in. Despairing of the whole episode, I went to hide upstairs in some hot water. On my way I noticed my other, older cat, fast asleep in the middle of his litter tray.

There has been more trouble on the stretch of train line at Dawlish in Devon, which seems to get bashed about by the sea every year. They could divert the train line inland but that would be far less fun, not least because you wouldn't get such elaborate excuses for train delays, my favourite of which remains: 'A wave has hit the train, which has knocked all the air out of it.'

My dad has been up north. 'BRADFORD WAS REALLY LITERARY,' he tells me. 'Really?' I say. 'I never thought of it as a particularly bookish city.' 'NOT LITERARY. LITTERY, YOU TWAZZOCK,' he replies.

I was at my local train station and heard an announcement that the train had been delayed. I wasn't getting a train but it still worried me.

There are two types of people in the world. People who fucking love maps, and people who don't.

The difference in driving culture in the South -est and the far side of East Anglia is more pronounced than a lot of people admit. The tiny lanes in the South West nurture a defensive driving outlook and a disregard for pristine paintwork. But in Norfolk many people view their cars as not so much an extension of their personality as the personality itself. Engine size and bodywork are inextricably tied in with who they believe they are becoming as an individual. They rev their engines and race you at the lights, never suspecting for a moment that you're not signed up for the same tournament as them;

you're just listening to a 1960s Gene Clark album and reminding yourself to buy lettuce. They make a risky move, without signalling, to gain one position in the queue, and you can't help speculating about what they believe they will achieve, and what prize awaits them at the end of their journey – a piece of food so delectable, perhaps, that placing it on the tongue thirty-nine seconds earlier will make all the difference. My car is often hungry, but doesn't join in, and probably couldn't even if it wanted to. One of the many questions I have answered 'Yes' to while living in Norfolk is 'Is your car actually just held together with tape?'

Strange how old people always seem younger when you know they have a living parent. In the lanes near my house, old ladies can often be seen helping their much older mums on their daily walks. They move extraordinarily slowly. If they walked all the way to the nearest town at this pace they wouldn't arrive until the middle of next year. The sight of it gets me somewhere deep in my diaphragm. Maybe it's the same old lady each time, and the same mum. If so, the one old lady and her even older mum are chameleonic, and they clearly like to experiment with different looks, to keep strangers like me on our toes.

I've been up north for a week, which has reminded me, amongst other things, that the Deep South-west of the UK is a country all of its own. 'How are you?' I say to the first person I see when I get back to Devon, my friend Ru. 'Great!' he tells me. 'I was up all night last night on Dartmoor with an Ecuadorian shaman.'

Text from my mum: 'Your dad asked the plumber yesterday if there was any gossip in the village. The plumber said, "YES! Pete Wilton's bull got out and mounted one of John Michael's cows and now she's pregnant!"'.

*

Wood pigeons in the garden are feasting on the lentils I left out last night, being periodically dive-bombed by rooks. In Hungary people eat lentils on New Year's Eve because they look like coins, and doing so is supposed to make you rich in the coming twelve months.

Someone once described me as 'part tree' and it remains the greatest compliment I have ever received.

My friend's girlfriend said she was going to draw me as my spirit animal but it was going to be a surprise. She came back with a drawing of me as a heron. Ever since then, I've had 'I'm every heron' go around in my head, to the tune of 'I'm Every Woman', every time I see a heron.

After stormy weather, the lanes in south Devon are scattered with damp, furry branches, and it's these that Billy, the small poodle I walk for my friend, likes to carry with him on our walks. Some are as much as twice the length of his body, and he guards them fiercely from me, as if remembering the time I cruelly stole one from him, then sold it, for hard cash. He instantly legitimises me as a walker, and the people we pass – especially those who also have dogs – are far more cheery in their hellos than they would be if he was not with me. But in truth I am far more of a threat when I'm with him: a potential chastiser of cattle and sheep, a de-calmer of rare birds. I make sure I'm at least as friendly in my greetings to those I pass who are alone, because a fact not remembered enough in the British countryside is that walkers without dogs are people too.

Somebody has been putting flowers on the Lorna Doone statue in Dulverton, and nobody knows who. Behind her, the River Barle runs down from Exmoor. Locals refer to the statue as 'The Barley Tart'.

I bought some flea treatment for my two cats. It said it was flea treatment you could use on house rabbits, too. The box warned that the flea treatment was not suitable for rabbits intended for human consumption. I had not realised anyone kept rabbits with the intention of eating them. Or maybe there are bands of insurrectionary folk who have been known to go out on renegade missions in the countryside, defleaing wild rabbits? This is the explanation I prefer.

Before the turnpike on the old road into the west, it would take four days for people to get from London to Exeter. Afterwards it took just sixteen and a half hours. I imagine it probably would have been even quicker than that, if everyone didn't always slow down to gawp at Stonehenge.

I was on a train to Bristol from Devon. It was busy. The man with the buffet trolley was talking about how difficult it was, getting between carriages, having to constantly reverse for people. 'It's pants, that's what this is,' said the buffet trolley operator. 'The train needs an upper level, I think that's yer problem,' said the customer. 'I should have got stuck in at school and made something of myself, that's my problem,' replied the buffet trolley operator. In front of me, a woman talking to her friend about perfume had a voice like a biscuit. A baby screamed and she told it to shut up, under her breath, still sounding like a biscuit.

Baby in Face: my future powerful memoir about people being unable to have full conversations with friends due to babies being shoved in their faces.

A Day Without Crisps: my raw, autobiographical novella based on the one day I actually managed to get through without having any crisps.

I walked further east and the soundtrack was horse clops and distant gunshots, the fat flick of rain on my anorak hood. Starlings gathering in trees looked from a distance like catkins and I went to meet them, watched by a row of cows bored out of their minds. The starlings took off in a funnel, then returned to their roost, not yet ready to murmurate – not for me, not for anyone. Rain swirled in from over the bare hill. 'MR CHIPS' said the lettering on an empty van behind a barn, surrounded by rusting agricultural machinery straight out of a *Robot Wars* scrapyard. Intransigent ivy suffocated old tractor tyres. I was late for my friends at the pub so I picked up my pace as I returned to the outskirts of the village, which made overheard conversations just fragments, frustrating in their splicedness. 'She's having a few problems right now because her shed blew down in the wind,' said a lady. 'And I said no, I'm not having any intimacy anywhere,' said another lady, further on, by the recreation ground.

*

I woke up towards 1 a.m. to the sound of a door banging downstairs and decided I was being burgled. Noises like this have happened before in similarly remote houses in the countryside and I've been wrong, but this time my assumption was correct: three badgers were attempting, fairly successfully, to get into the metal box where I keep seed for my garden birds. One was holding the lid of the metal box open while the other attempted to pull the birdseed bag out with its teeth and the third stood watch. They scattered, but not quickly, and I felt vulnerable in my naked state, thinking about badger attack stories I'd heard in the past and been a little dismissive about.

'PUT SEASHELLS IN THE ANKLES OF YOUR SOCKS,' my dad told me. 'Why on earth would I do that?' I asked. 'YOUR MUM TOLD ME YOU'VE GOT BADGERS IN THE GARDEN. WHEN THEY BITE YOUR LEG, THEY'LL CRUNCH ON THE SHELLS AND THINK THEY'VE ALREADY HIT BONE, THEN LEAVE YOU ALONE.'

I drove across country and listened to Bob Dylan's audiobook. I loved picturing the young Dylan arriving in New York at his record company for the first time, full of talent and tall tales of dead parents and his freight train journey there from the Midwest. I also loved hearing his thoughts on his late sixties recluse period, which should probably be mandatory listening for anybody under the misapprehension that celebrity is a desirable condition. Afterwards

I listened to all of *Highway 61 Revisited*, and all of *Blood on the Tracks*, and the 50% of *Blonde on Blonde* that I can cope with, realising that the book was permitting me to enjoy them on a new level, but also thinking that the use of language on them, at their best, made the use of language in the book seem kind of pedestrian. By this point I had again passed South Mimms, where I decided not to get a coffee, and where ten years and one month ago I'd dropped off two excitable buskers who were on their way from Norfolk to Cornwall to pick apples and play music on the street. I wondered about the buskers, who would probably be pushing thirty now, and hoped they were still making music, and that that summer still seemed as recent in their minds as it did to me, rather than something ancient and unreachable, from another, looser life. I could still remember so much about that weekend – the gig I saw in London that evening and the conversation I had with my friend Emma after it; the immense skill and determination of the disabled man I played golf with the next day in Hampshire; the smell of the stew my friend Jackie cooked me at her house in Pembrokeshire that night; the photo Jackie took of me in her garden the next day with her dog and cat where I looked oddly like a late 1970s DJ on the cusp of decline – but that was less due to the power of my memory and more due to the fact that the decade between thirty-four and forty-four is not as long as a decade is when you're younger.

The M5, southbound. The service stations zipped by: Sedgemoor, where one summer they had to open a second car park, due to its popularity. Taunton Deane, where I once burned my mouth on a pasty, then, seconds later, due to extreme hunger, forgot, and burned my mouth on the pasty again. There are some people you see at service stations that you don't see in any other part of British life. Perhaps they live there? I'd been away from Devon for a while, living in a harsh place. Not that long, really, but it felt like longer, because it was winter, and because of that harshness. I saw the 'Welcome to Devon' sign then tasted a tear on my lip, before I'd even realised the tear had fallen from my eye. Moments before, I'd seen the Wellington Monument on the left side of my car, which always seemed to be surrounded by mist, and always made me feel better when it was on the left side of my car, rather than the right. I left again, somehow, due to a series of intricate circumstances. Then I came back. I couldn't stop coming back. As I came back the latest time, and passed the monument, I mentally went over the stuff I might attach to the wall of a new house. There was scaffolding on the monument made it look like a giant rawl plug, up there in the mist on the hill.

TROUT WITHOUT EMOTION

I like trespassing, and get increasing pleasure out of quietly doing the opposite of what authority tells me to, so when I read about the tiny, little-known Cornish cove, and I got there, and saw a sign saying the footpath to the little-known, tiny Cornish cove was closed, and that a wire fence had been erected where the entrance to the path to the tiny Cornish cove was, I climbed over the fence, walked along the path and swam at the tiny Cornish cove. On the cliffs directly above, during the First World War, my friend's great-grandfather had taken off over the sea in a propeller plane he'd personally helped to build. It took three or four failed attempts before he managed it, and the whole village came out to watch and cheer.

The big lie about talent is that it's something innately already there, something 'natural', rather than something that comes from doing something so many times, at such a self-punishing and tiring level, that you can't fail to finally be decent at it.

*

My dad has come to an arrangement with the public pool in Nottinghamshire where he swims: after everyone else has got out of the pool, he is permitted to do a somersault before he gets changed. 'THEY OPEN UP THE STORAGE CUPBOARD AND LET ME GO IN THERE SO I CAN GET A GOOD RUN-UP,' he said. Last week my dad, who will be seventy in August, got his friend Malcolm, who is seventy-three, to film the somersault. 'It's shattered all his illusions,' my mum told me. 'Until he saw the film he thought he was creating poetry in motion. But it's really just an old bloke who can't run fast doing a sideways flop.'

I am swimming in the local lido today when my neighbour Becca spots me and wanders over. 'Tom!' she says, placing a Tupperware container at the side of the pool. 'There are some steamed salmon chunks here. My cat Pushkin has very expensive taste and has suddenly decided he doesn't like them anymore. I wondered if yours might like them.' I thank her profusely, and carry on smoothly with my front crawl, as, perhaps more impressively, do the three other swimmers around me who have witnessed our exchange.

Message from my mum: 'Your dad is back from swimming with some frogspawn. His friend had left it in the changing room for him.'

The story is that once, in town, someone had broken their leg and just as their stretcher was being wheeled into an ambulance, watched by a small crowd of people, a man came running through the crowd, waving his arms. 'WAIT!' he said. 'I am a holistic therapist.' Nobody knows when it happened or can verify for sure that it did but everyone I have met – even those who work in the sphere of holistic therapy – wants to believe it's true.

*

Young people are constantly remarking on the process of getting another year older, how shocking it is, as if they'd believed it would never happen. Old people rarely remark on it. It's no longer surprising to them.

Everyone has their own individual sneeze and it's very important to be comfortable with that. Never try to sneeze like somebody else. It will totally fuck you up.

Ageing: the condition of becoming less serious about all you were once far too serious about and more serious about all that you once undervalued.

Directly prior to death, I am certain, there is an anteroom where you are reunited with all the socks you once knew. My sock drawer is like a diverse but unsuccessful sock dating site: socks of every shape and colour, each of them alone, failing to find love. It never occurred to me until recently that it was OK to wear odd socks, that nobody would report me to a governing body for it. This is no doubt in part influenced by a couple of ex-partners: one, in particular, who admitted that seeing the wearing of odd socks sent her tumbling into a minor state of rage. Although I didn't share it, this irrational dislike was one of those small flaws – such as her equally strong distaste for the wearing of watches – that made me love her a little bit more. In the summer of 2013, when we were out for lunch with my American friends Albert and Lara and their children Matthew and Nathaniel, who were seven and nine at the time, we all talked about her dislike of odd socks. Seeing the four of them is always something that lifts my mood, not least because listening to Matthew and Nathaniel talk has, right from when they were very small, been more entertaining than listening to most expensively priced comedy gigs by adults. But we didn't catch up with them for about five months after that. When they arrived at my house the next time we saw them, the first thing Matthew and Nathaniel did was lift up their trouser legs to show my girlfriend the odd socks they were both wearing.

I went to the pub with my parents. A waitress left her notepad and pen on the table and my dad immediately began to sketch a man sitting two tables away. My mum pointed out the trout on the menu and said it sounded nice and I said that I was full vegetarian now, not just pescatarian. 'TROUT DON'T HAVE FEELINGS,' said my dad. 'THEY'VE PROVED IT.'

I'm no hard-line hippie where natural medicine is concerned but sometimes simple home cures work. I had a skin tag on my eyelid. It was annoying, possibly even a bit worrying. I prevaricated about getting it looked at. Time went on, and it didn't go away. Two, three years. One day I put on a new sweater and the price tag caught the skin tag and knocked it off my eyelid. That was six years ago, and it hasn't come back.

Isn't it amazing the way life can seem too short and intrinsically magical, yet at the same time feel like a long, uphill road, potholed with fuckwits.

Ginger beer is a great drink to drink if you feel like you haven't coughed enough recently.

If anyone enjoys the taste of old microphones, heartburn and dust, I highly recommend M&S hand-cooked parmesan, asparagus and truffle crisps.

COFFEE REVIEW: Tesco Finest Colombian Supremo. Overtones of fudge pantry. Notes of a shelf bought in 2007. Lingering raspberry sadness. 6/10

COFFEE REVIEW: Cafédirect Machu Picchu. Punchy hints of old sledge. Fruity top notes of damp trousers. Aftertaste of village let-down. 1/10

I tire of hand-cooked crisps. They don't excite me. Crisps cooked by the assured steel talons of robot hawks would at least make a nice change. Expensive crisps do nothing for me. Crisps are the most subversive snack because they rewrite the established rules of food pricing: the cheaper you go, the better the taste. There is a lower limit to this rule, however, as the packet of Aldi Monster Claws my friend Andrew bought me as a house-warming present demonstrated.

*

It's not true that breakfast is the most important meal of the day. The most important meal of the day is curry.

A solid cooking rule to follow is to remember that when recipes say 'add two cloves of garlic', it's always a misprint and what they actually mean is six.

At twenty it doesn't matter how you sleep, you look the same. When you're over thirty-five sleep has the power to make you look any age from twenty-three to eighty-six.

Message from my dad: 'ON SUNDAY I AXED OFF A BIT OF MY FINGER AND PUT IT TO ONE SIDE JUST IN CASE BUT WHEN I LOOKED ROUND A BIRD HAD EATEN IT.'

I've got some shirts I was so, so excited about when I bought them. Sometimes, when I'm wondering what to wear, I put one of them on, then go, 'Neh.' That's been happening for a whole decade with a couple of them, and I really need to let them go. There's nothing wrong with the shirts. It's not like the shirts dislike me, or I dislike them. The shirts and I are just different people with different opinions.

The epiphany now hits me that I have spent my entire life preparing to be the age I am at any given point.

A friend and I were on a long walk and were agreeing about loads of stuff. One of the things we agreed on was that we hated liars, and it felt like an important and bonding moment at the time that marked us out as two of a particular kind of person but later it felt a bit less important and unique because there are probably very few people out there who would say, 'You know what I really like? Liars. They're great.'

Nobody told me I'd still want to dance, pretty much all the time, by the time I reached my forty-fourth January. Nobody told me I'd feel better now about my mind and body than I have during my entire adult life. Nobody told me I'd get more out of music, even more than I did when I was seventeen and regularly threw myself into mosh pits. Nobody told me how great it was to come through the back gate of an unfamiliar village churchyard in midwinter while a pile of leaves smouldered in a nearby garden. Nobody told me that, when buying tortilla chips, it's best to go for the absolute cheapest range. Nobody told me all that much. But why should they?

I've been over at my friend Amy's. Her very Christian neighbours have named their Wi-Fi network 'Jesus Loves You'. Her other neighbours have responded by naming theirs 'Satan's Information Hole'.

I reached consciousness just as the first rays of dawn lit the room, and the first sound I heard was a gull squawking in my hallway. Because the night had been hot, I had left the back door of my house open, and I now regretted it, as it had allowed the gull to enter my kitchen and dining room, spraying its wet faeces all over plates and cupboards and rugs. But then I remembered it was probably not a gull, but my cat Ralph, who, like so many other individuals who have spent a lifetime singing, has been experiencing voice problems in old age, often meowing totally silently, but sometimes making a croaky noise evocative of a small, unhappy seabird. I fed Ralph and my other, more officious cat, Roscoe, who danced into my hand. I listened to 'Peace Frog' by The Doors while I cleaned my teeth, and danced, but not into anyone's hand.

*

Something a lot of people will tell you about art is that genius can't be rushed. What is less often pointed out is that non-genius also can't be rushed. Tea, snacks, naps and idle moments staring out of windows are not exclusive to geniuses. Each of us deserves our fair quota of them.

Everyone was called John this month. It's like that, some months. I had lunch with my friend John, who isn't driving at present, after suffering a mysterious blackout and crashing his car into a wall in late summer. When he opened his eyes after the blackout, the front half of the car was dangling precariously over a twelve-foot precipice. 'It was like the final scene in *The Italian Job*,' he said. An elderly pedestrian, who had witnessed the crash, scuttled over and sat in the back seat, behind John and John's wife Polly, to help even the weight out until the rescue team arrived. I sold some records to my friend John in Bristol and accompanied him to a screening of a documentary about drugs, which prompted me to read Aldous Huxley's writing about drugs. My mum, visiting that week, told me about John, a family friend from Langley Mill in Derbyshire with a wrestling background, who recently witnessed a thug threatening a cafe owner in London with a knife, and calmly marched over and took the knife out of his hands. 'I'll tell you what knives are for: cutting bread,' he told the thug, then sat down and resumed eating his chips.

You can tell a lot about people from the way they act in a car park. People who reverse into a space in a car park tend to be people who like to forward plan very carefully. They book holidays and haircuts long in advance and never have empty tanks for their oil-fired central heating or run out of salt or non-bio washing liquid. I never reverse into a space in a car park.

*

Message from mum: 'We've got mice living here. Your dad's not happy. They've stolen all the chocolate he hides under the sofa cushion.'

*

I go to the gym but I don't go to the gym, and never would. My current gym is the second gym I have joined solely for the swimming pool, ignoring the other facilities and declining the offer of a tour of them upon enrolment. As I walk through the car park, and past reception, I feel sterilised and numbed: by music, by smells, by light, by the big screen near the entrance and the strange seating area which feels like a departure lounge for an airport without any planes. But it's the coldest part of winter and I don't get in the river or sea in the coldest part of winter. I reached the poolside last week, and was relieved to see the water was empty, as the pool had been busy lately. As usual, there were lots of people congregated around the pool edge, chatting, using the hot tub, going from the sauna to the steam room. Still, it was surprising, seeing the pool entirely empty on a weekend afternoon. 'I wouldn't get in if I were you,' said a woman heading in the direction of the steam room. 'Someone's just been sick in it.'

The reason I swim is never the first twenty-five lengths. It's something that kicks in after that, usually not until length thirty-two or thirty-three; an elemental zone I go into, where I stop getting in my own way mentally and everything is watery and simple. For the first twenty-five lengths or more, I'm still straightening myself out, prone to old bad habits. I kick from the knee, or don't get enough width on my weaker left side. But there's a trance feeling later on when I'm in a medium gear, sliding through the water, that I could permit to carry on forever. It's far more meditative than any formal meditation has ever been for me. It's easier than it once was because, when I started moving more effectively, it made me quicker, which meant that I could do more in the same space of time than I once could, which made my muscles more toned, which made me move even more effectively, and so on, forever. At its best, it's like the direct opposite of a vicious circle, and it makes me suspect that my swimming guru, Charlie Loram, and his mentor, Steven Shaw, might be touched with a sprinkling of genius. Doing this for nine months – plus the less intensive swimming I did for the years leading up to that – has brought me to the point where the reason I swim is not primarily because of swimming's benefits or recuperative aspects; it's for the experience itself, which is the part of my day I have started to look forward to as much as any other. But I know that could change. Because that's another reason I swim: it heightens my awareness that everything is shifting all the time, and makes me more open to it. In a year, the reason I swim could be totally different. And that's OK.

The angry postman came this morning, not the friendly postman, or the friendly postlady, who sadly very rarely works this route. The angry postman delivered a record I'd bought second-hand with the name of its previous owner written across the middle of it in rub-down transfer lettering. I used to forge strong bonds with postmen, back in another life. There was Dave, who was medium-sized and white and who talked a lot about Deep Purple, and ended up inviting me for a round of golf. Then there was other Dave, who was small and black and worked in Nottingham and loved northern soul and used to come into my living room for a breather from his round in the Trent Bridge area and listen to Aretha Franklin with me. It's like a different postal planet to the one I live on now. I always know the angry postman is here because he knocks really, really loudly before he rings my doorbell, which he must realise by now is a loud doorbell. I don't know if it's something he does at every house, or if it's some kind of passive-aggressive vendetta, dating back to, say, one possible morning in July when it was obvious I was in because he could just hear some flute coming from my living-room speakers and see a light burning but maybe I didn't hear him because I was in the shower. I always thank the angry postman for my mail but he never says a word as he hands it to me. Maybe something horrible has happened to him recently. Maybe he has an angry postman too. I notice that I feel a fair bit worse about the world after I've been handed my mail by the angry postman, just as I notice I feel a fair bit better about it when I have been handed my mail by the nice postman or postlady, or had a chat with somebody who works in a shop or a cafe or a pub who seems in a genuinely bright mood and curious about their environment. All these little invisible rods of energy, good and bad and indifferent, are being passed between humans like little red-hot and ice-cold and lukewarm relay batons every day, altering our moods, perhaps even significantly changing the path of our lives. But we pretend they aren't there. We pretend it's only the big stuff making us happy or sad: love, new life, houses, death, career, heartbreak. Sometimes it's not. Sometimes it's just a stranger smiling and saying good morning while they hand you a VG+ record you bought off Discogs that used to belong to someone called Pam who owned a Letraset in the 1970s.

*

If I had a pound for every James Joyce novel I'd read, I'd have thirteen pence.

The most important job of a record dealer is not, as is popularly believed, to keep clean, well-organised stock and price it fairly; it is to have the right kind of stickers. Even in the enlightened age we now live in, some record dealers still use stickers which, after only a day attached to a record, will bring a large chunk of the cover art off with them. These dealers probably don't think they are doing anything wrong and wonder why their customers don't return to buy more vinyl. I will tell you the answer: it is because their customers are too busy making voodoo dolls of them, then burning the dolls on fires in occult poison broths, along with old rats and the saliva of toads. A sticker on a record tends not to have the charm of a former owner's pen mark on a record – a rare exception being the tiny yellow sticker saying 'Keith' that somebody has stuck on Keith Richards' shoulder on my copy of *Out of Our Heads* by The Rolling Stones. People have very occasionally accused me of being a serious record collector but they're wrong. One way you can tell I'm not a serious record collector is that until a few years back I still had price stickers on some of my records, and not just ones that I'd kept on them intentionally because they were from the 1960s and 1970s and had comically low amounts of American currency written on them. The main reason I no longer have price stickers on my records is because at a party in 2013 my more conscientious record-collecting friend Steve, horrified at my neglect, went through the whole lot and, with the most remarkable level of expert care, peeled every one of them off. 'Steve, come over here and have some of this lemon drizzle cake and play Giant Jenga,' other guests began to say to Steve, an hour or two after he had begun to peel off the stickers. 'I am almost done – five more minutes!' replied Steve, but he was not telling the truth. Due to the extreme level of his concentration, he had become inaccurate and unrealistic about time.

Nottingham was once described as 'the worst slum in the British Empire outside India'. If you visit Rob's Records, in Hurts Yard, just down from Upper Parliament Street, you will discover that it can still be very dirty, even to this day.

A few years ago I had an extremely boring but significant dream. In the dream, I was with some close friends, flicking through some racks of vinyl in an unspecified record shop. Nothing else happened. The dream had a serene, aquatic quality, very ambient and undramatic. But what the dream made me realise, at a point when I was buying very few records, was that hunting for records makes me happy, even though it's fairly pointless. The fact is, once you start looking hard into a lot of things that make you happy, you can easily construct the argument that they are fairly pointless too. Since that point I've not gone out of my way to stop myself buying records, and have mourned several that I sold in my twenties. But I think a record collection is allowed to be a constantly shape-shifting beast. When you have listened to a lot of records, for a lot of years, a kind of honing organically happens, whether you're pruning a collection or not: a more intense understanding of what you adore, a deeper honesty regarding what is vital. It's happened to me recently with books, too. So long as the same fine-tuning doesn't double as a situation where you're closed off to change or a new kind of delight, I think it's a positive process. Modern life is overwhelming. Culture is overwhelming, especially if you're interested in a lot of different stuff from a lot of different places. There is endless very accessible good music and art and literature in the world. It's unrealistic to strive to cram every bit of it into your house, even though at times it can be very tempting. Not long ago I sold about 500 of my records to fund a cross-country house move. I selected them slowly and carefully and, so far, I haven't missed any of them. A bystander might argue that I had a few too many records, and I would be very willing to chat this out with them, potentially agreeing with at least 80% of where they are coming from. Around the time I was selling my records, I also gradually discovered that I'd lost about £600 of other records to warping due to my neglecting to keep them properly covered up on sunny days in my last house's insanely hot, glass-dominated living room. That hurt me in a soft vulnerable place beyond my skin that nobody can see, and with hindsight I did quite well not to fall onto the floor in a heap and cry, but I'm slowly recovering emotionally and hope that I might financially soon, too. A record collection is always a story. The question is what kind. You can let the story keep expanding, like some epic work of fiction written by a writer so famous and intimidating that their editor is too scared to be honest and tell them they need to get a grip and rein it in a bit. Or you can continue pruning and shaping the story, keeping it as honest as possible. I'm tending more towards the latter approach. But then I am a person who is passionate about editing: I regard it as one of my top six parts of writing, along with faffing, researching, thinking, eating and typing. I like the music of Kevin Ayers but I don't like the music of Kevin Ayers as much as other people have told me to like the music of Kevin Ayers, so, in the interest of honesty, I have recently removed the small Kevin Ayers chapter from my story. Also: selling records means I can afford to buy more records, and I don't want to stop buying records. I don't want to say, at the point where I am now in my life as a music lover, 'OK. That's it. I'm finished. The story is done.'

*

There is no concrete best song ever. The best song ever is an ever-shifting concept, coloured by weather, hope, disappointment and the moon. Actually, that's bullshit. It's 'Unhooked Generation' by Freda Payne.

The Vinyl Resting Place was a large wooden shed full of vinyl that I discovered close to the Suffolk coast in 2013 while on my way to the sunken port of Dunwich to listen for underwater ghost bells and look for mythical sea creatures. I did not find any mythical sea creatures but I did find a copy of the first Dick Gaughan LP for the same price that some people will happily pay for a glorified cheese cob. The Vinyl Resting Place was owned by JJ, a retired session musician who'd always wanted his own record shop and, upon being diagnosed with a terminal illness, had decided to finally open one. A few weeks later, I returned with my friends Dan, Amy and Seventies Pat, half expecting to discover only an ordinary shed filled with rakes, spades and bradawls and realise with a depressing bump back down to earth that I had dreamed the whole episode. But the Vinyl Resting Place was still there, more colourfully stuffed with wares than ever. I stood back selflessly and let my friends search the racks ahead of me, then spent the rest of the afternoon, seething about the smart-looking original pressing of Bert Jansch's *Jack Orion* LP that Seventies Pat found for only eight quid.

People who say they hate the Beatles are lying.

I rewatched a couple of Beatles documentaries, including *Living in the Material World*, Martin Scorsese's 2011 film about George Harrison. I noticed, again, that all four Beatles shared precisely the same hair colour for the first two-thirds of the sixties, until Lennon's got lighter, and the three most important ones were almost precisely the same height. People argue endlessly about who the best Beatle was and their choice normally says much more about them than the Beatle they are talking about, but every year it seems increasingly preposterous to claim that any other solo album by a Beatle is better than Harrison's *All Things Must Pass*, from 1970. I relistened to Harrison's subsequent seventies albums after watching the documentary and keenly willed them to be better than they are. I also couldn't help looking up the full version of Ringo and George's 1988 interview on *Aspel & Company*, from which we see a short spliced clip in *Living in the Material World*. It's not comfortable viewing. George is patient and quiet and reluctant and wry, and Ringo is that combination of quick-witted and massively boorish that naturally funny people, when very drunk, often are. Ringo's hair looks like he's used it to clean the extractor hood on a tired cooker in a bad canteen. George doesn't look particularly good either, but only because it's 1988, and nobody looked good in 1988. Sometimes it's astonishing to think people managed to find each other attractive enough to have sex in 1988, in the same way that it's astonishing to think people managed to find each other attractive enough to have sex in the 1300s, when nobody used toothpaste or bathed regularly. If you watch the *Aspel & Company* clip on YouTube, you might also get a box to your right suggesting you also watch Harrison's 1971 interview with Dick Cavett, in which Harrison's hair, beard and clothes look utterly fantastic. Everyone likes to believe every change in their hair and outfit is a step forward, yet sometimes seventeen years of apparent stylistic steps forward, with no financial restrictions, can somehow lead you to a backcombed ex-rocker mullet and a light grey suit that looks like it came from the sale rack in Littlewoods. What's bewildering about the mid-to-late eighties is not the way people who looked brilliant and made mind-blowing music in the sixties and seventies started dressing and overproducing their music, it's the fact that they clearly viewed it all as progress. Even George, a pop star more impervious to fads than most, wasn't impervious to this. What's common to both interviews – and all of *Living in the Material World* – is an awareness that George is the one Beatle who never came across as an inverted commas version of himself. 'I'm even more normal than normal people,' he tells Aspel. I don't quite believe that, but I do believe that he lived a fantastic, spiritually rich life, as true to himself and bullshit-free as his situation permitted. He also feels amazingly familiar, and not just in a way that all likeable famous people you've been aware of your whole life feel familiar. I think it could be a Scouse thing. I'm not from Liverpool but most of my family are, and, as my Liverpudlian friend Andrew claims, Scouseness runs deeper than actually growing up there; it's hereditary.

It's high summer in the South-west: calming and beatific in every way, with the exception of the panic of wanting to hold onto the moment, and knowing it will soon be slipping away. Last night I was at a party in a field, next to a house made entirely out of found objects. In Devon in July, there's always a party in a field somewhere nearby, and it's not hard to get an invite. A big fire. Lots of long rough-wool cardigans and productless hair. The moon was hanging full over the hedge and people were talking about it and how it was altering their mood, the friends who were acting crazy in the last couple of days because of it. A lady with a huge amount of hair took a seat next to me. She was barefoot but had a pair of socks in a wicker basket which she explained were 'for later when it gets cold'. I was driving so I went to the bar and asked for a water. The man behind it – tanned, wiry, fiftyish, in a Bob Marley t-shirt – told me they didn't have any. 'But here's an alternative,' he said, handing me four ice cubes. 'Hold these and wait five minutes.'

A carful of us were on the way to a festival, and it was a small festival, in quite a rural bit of Somerset, so there weren't a lot of signs leading to it, and after a while when the lanes got quieter we started to wonder if we'd gone wrong somewhere, and Mel suggested we stop the car and ask the man at the side of the road, but when we stopped we realised he was a scarecrow, not a man. I blamed myself for our mistake. I have seen a lot of scarecrows and because of that like to think I've become good at distinguishing them from real men.

*

As someone who has spent almost his entire life living in various parts of the British countryside, I can confirm that the area between Glastonbury and Castle Cary contains the strongest rural smells in the country. It goes through waves, but the main smell is not manure, more slurry; it's salty, industrial, laced with manufactured cow. There have been days recently when the smell coming off the fields around my house has been so strong, it has permeated everything: my house, my bedclothes, my cats, my fresh washing, my hair, the very fabric of my being.

Drunk people rarely make good romantic choices. The problem is where the drinking takes place. Bookshops, that's where people should drink.

Is the utter appallingness of my short-term memory a price I pay for the weird, random brilliance of my long-term memory? I am starting to think so. As my short-term memory becomes increasingly haywire, my long-term memory only strengthens; one day, I fear, I will misplace every cup of tea I make, not remember to text any friends back at all but recall the events of 1993 in their entirety. Short-term memory and long-term memory are so different in their motives. Short-term memory latches onto one negative in a sea of positive and torments you with it. Long-term memory is a snob, a perfectionist, turning so-so summers into an intoxicating psychedelic montage. Even when you properly learn this, and try to account for it, it's still a snob. 2010, for example, is now far enough away to be part of my long-term memory, which has decided that it was a year without a winter, or at least without any of winter's drawbacks, where I did nothing but meet interesting new people, hold a party at my house every week, walk every footpath in Norfolk and Suffolk and drink beer twice a week in my garden with friends when it was warm, or, when it was cold, in our favourite pub where the log fire was always burning and our favourite woodworm-infested old bench at the back was mysteriously always free, as if we were characters in some unlikely Norfolk sitcom. Long-term memory has conveniently removed from the picture fortnight-long head colds, speeding tickets, a painful blood clot, the person I liked who didn't like me back, the person who liked me who I didn't like back, a spell of creative block, Internet trolls, money terror. I knew it was very important to try to remember that in deciding to move back to the county where I lived during that year and had such a good time. You can't have the 2010 of your long-term memory back because you can't have any year back, but also because that 2010 wasn't quite real; it was just an angle, created by a director with some fancy technology who wants to keep your attention. Also, the pub has new owners now, and new seats. It's lost all its soul. We don't go there anymore.

Mist is rising up, gathering around the trunks of trees. The weather is that special quiet you only get at dusk, as if it needs not to be disturbed while it has a think about what it's going to do tonight.

I'm suspicious of success. How can you not be? Success, as popularly defined, is when everything is going well, and that's when you tend to announce – even if it's only to yourself – 'Everything is going well!' or 'I feel great!' which is like pressing a button wired directly to the unlock function on a door, behind which a series of bad events have been sitting patiently, waiting for a reason to happen. Success is a trap. A lot of bands have made a lot of astonishingly bad records at a point in their career when they're considered very successful. The trick, I often think, is to stay a comfortable distance beneath success. But even then you're not infallible. Success will lure you in with some of the stuff it promises, even if you're not interested in the success itself. I can sometimes get conned into thinking I've become interested in achieving success, when what I've in fact become interested in is the idea of selling enough books to feel a little bit more stable and secure about my future. And when I take a step back I'm not even sure I'm interested in that. Of all the activities of the modern age that have been proven to help books sell more, the only one I'm truly interested in doing is writing more books. And I am very aware that a lot of the energy of the book I've just completed, and loved writing so so much, comes from uncertainty: the increasingly peripatetic nature of my life, the doubt about whether I'm still going to be able to afford to do this in a year or two, the nowness of it. I recently went through the brief delusion that I might be able to buy a house as a way of feeling a moderate extra bit of security and reducing my monthly outgoings, before I looked at my recent earnings and the cold hard facts of what it actually takes to get a mortgage these days and threw the idea out of the window, cackling maniacally at what a fool I had been. Do I live in a chaotic, financially precarious, impulsive way because I write the books I write, or do I write the books I write because I live in a chaotic, financially precarious, impulsive way? It's become quite hard to tell. This semi-nomadic life I am living, going from place to place and writing about my environment, living quietly with few commitments and no boss, being able to do nothing much more than guess about the future, came about slightly by accident. It can be tiring and impractically expensive, feel – at the bad times – like a gradual haemorrhaging of my future, but so much of it is so very enjoyable, especially in a creative sense, so I will carry on with it for now and see where it takes me next.

Thomas Paine, the author of *Rights of Man*, lived on a hill – one of Norfolk's few – known as 'the Wilderness' when he was growing up. It was distinguished topographically by being directly opposite the local gallows. The house was not far from where I went to live, two and a half centuries later. Next door but one lived a hairdresser, who fell out with her son. In revenge, he opened a rival hair salon, which became more successful than his mum's.

*

The dawn chorus is so sweet in April but by October it's just six drunk rooks arguing in a dead tree.

My dad said he touched another man on the street yesterday, very gently, without the other man realising. 'IT WAS THE

MATERIAL ON HIS SUIT,' he said. 'IT LOOKED LOVELY AND I COULDN'T RESIST HAVING A FEEL.' He was in London, where he'd met a Komodo dragon, which he thought was called Roger, but discovered was called Raja only after he had addressed the Komodo dragon several times as Roger. Later, he talked about my grandma, who was always very aware of the worst things that could happen in any situation, and would not let him wash knives as a child. On the street in the council estate where my dad grew up, my grandma once found two of the boys from across the road fighting in front of her and my granddad's house. 'Are you making love?' she asked the boys, and they let go of one another and retreated indoors.

A green woodpecker is on my lawn. It hasn't seen me. It's looking around, very cautiously, like somebody with very expensive clothes who knows they are elusive.

A lot of people think insects are out to make their life difficult but they're not – they're just being insects. Flying ants don't live long, so while they do, it's not fair to deny them their right to party.

Being ultimately an optimist, I will generally claim not to have regrets, owing to the fact I have internally rebranded them as useful experiences. But one I find hard to do that with is the fact that I didn't keep regular notebooks and diaries for over three decades of my life, which is only a useful experience in the sense that it made me better at keeping notebooks and diaries after that. One of the reasons I want to read old notebooks and diaries is that I want to find out quite mundane stuff about my immediate environment at the time: how much stuff cost, what I did in an average day, what I ate. Today I ate the dusty end of a box of Dorset muesli (which is dusty, even though people say it isn't, although admittedly not as dusty as the end of the packet of most mueslis) with some blueberries on top, some onion bread-type stuff and tomatoes for lunch, then for dinner threw together an omelette with pretty much all the leftovers I had in the fridge. The latter tasted astoundingly good even though I damaged it a bit when I flipped it. I hold butter, rather than my own culinary skill, responsible. I went to see an excellent chiropractor in Wincanton who prodded and jerked me in lots of helpful ways. The appointment cost £32. I posted half-a-dozen signed copies of my new hardback at Wincanton post office, which I could only tell was a post office because it said 'Post Office' outside and had some scales. The weather is just getting slightly cooler, after several days of perfect blue skies shining down on LSD leaves. Insects are still quite confused. A shield bug flew through my living-room window and landed on Pentangle's *Reflection* LP, which I had somehow ranked in my head as the weakest Pentangle LP – something that isn't true, because there is no weak Pentangle LP. Every Pentangle LP is perfect, even in its small flaws. The photos of Pentangle on the inner gatefold cover of *Reflection* – the particular combination of hair and knitwear and winter coats and the washed-out green-brown light – always remind me of the way another, less well-known, now sadly defunct folk band looked when I met them in a pub in Caxton in Cambridgeshire during the researching of a feature I was writing on them for a newspaper which, out of all the features for newspapers I didn't end up actually writing, was definitely the one I spent most time on and was most disappointed not to write. That is now twelve years ago and that fact hits me hard because I feel I could open the door of that pub now and the band would still look the same, be the same, have the same jumpers. *Reflection* is next to me now. I'm writing this sitting on the squeaky 1970s leather sofa I bought remarkably cheaply a year and a half ago at an auction in Bristol, but should be at a standing desk, because that's what the chiropractor said would be best for my back. My black and white cat Roscoe has just come in, spooked, having been chased by a new neighbourhood cat that looks like a fatter-headed, meaner-eyed version of her. I'm reading the at-times heart-stoppingly sad *In Camden Town* by David Thomson, from 1983: a book about a part of the UK I thought I wasn't very interested in, but am now, because a great writer can make any place or subject interesting. I am carrying around with me today a feeling that I know too many people, which is one I didn't begin to carry around with me until about seven years ago, but am carrying a concomitant feeling that I don't want to stop myself getting to know more people. Even though it's not technically true, I feel like I've done nothing but reply to messages since I woke up, yet I'm heading to bed with a feeling of guilt about all the people I haven't texted, emailed or called, as I so often do.

When you're a kid, your parents tell you the best stories. Sometimes it's just the same when you're an adult. The best true short story I have ever been told is probably this one, from my mum: 'One day when you were a child, and we were living on a country lane, there was a knock on the door. I answered it, and waiting behind the door was a pantomime horse. Without uttering a word, the pantomime horse then turned and trotted away, and I went back inside and cooked your tea.'

I walked near Sherborne. It was my ninth long country walk of the month. A fire extinguisher was lodged in a hedge, far from anywhere there might be any obvious potential use for a fire extinguisher. The wind was strong and had a sharp doom-metal taste that it almost never has in the South-west. The sky was in the process of getting very clean; the kind of clean that happens when you wash art equipment with oil. My route took me past Sherborne Castle, the former home of Sir Walter Raleigh, whose embalmed head was kept around by his wife after his execution, for company, and also presumably the memories. I counted at least four gatehouses within the grounds – five, if you include the one without the gate. I can't imagine why you'd ever need that many. The wind felt like the kind of wind that comes to tidy up, so we can all move on.

ACKNOWLEDGEMENTS

This is the fourth book I have crowdfunded with Unbound which means, I suppose, that it's now become 'the norm' for me – but it's important that I remind myself that, as recently as a decade ago, that norm could never have happened. I almost certainly couldn't have persuaded a mainstream, traditional publisher to take a chance on *Notebook*, and, with no alternative available, it and its three predecessors would have remained an idealistic, niche dream. This is a book written by me, but made real by the power of a largeish group of enthusiastic people, as opposed to the power of a small group of people, whose enthusiasm, if it existed, might likely be driven by trends and fiscal targets. if you're among that largeish enthusiastic group of people, I cannot thank you enough. Big thanks also to my agent Ed Wilson and all the team at Unbound who have helped to put it together: Imogen Denny, Martha Sprackland, Hayley Shepherd, Mathew Clayton, Julian Mash, John Mitchinson, Caitlin Harvey, Georgia Odd and Catherine Emery. Thanks to Dave

Holwill and Matt Shaw for the website help. Thank you to Clare Melinsky for more wonderful psychedelic cover art and one of my favourite-ever ink hedgehogs, and to my parents, Jo and Mick, for their fantastic illustrations inside (I've collaborated with my mum before but this is the first time all three of us have worked together on a project). Finally, thank you to Geoff and her tough gang of cows, for waiting patiently for almost a decade while I harshly edited them out of three other books before deciding that this one was their chance to shine.

Unbound is the world's first crowdfunding publisher, established in 2011.

We believe that wonderful things can happen when you clear a path for people who share a passion. That's why we've built a platform that brings together readers and authors to crowdfund books they believe in – and give fresh ideas that don't fit the traditional mould the chance they deserve.

This book is in your hands because readers made it possible. Everyone who pledged their support, except those who wished to remain anonymous, is listed below. Join them by visiting unbound. com and supporting a book today.

Stacy Bennett
Sue Bentley
Christopher
   Bergedahl
JoAnna Berry
Mary Bettuchy
Suchada Bhiromb
   hakdi
Heather Binsch
Maggie Birchall
Deborah Black
Emma Blades
John Blythe
Meryl Boardman
Meda Bock-Brown
Ali Bodin
David Body
Caroline Bolton
Gilly Bolton
Steven Bond
Christen Boniface
Alex Booer
Jeannie Borsch
Joyce Boss
Michelle Bourg
Lesley Bourke
Polly Bowden
Teresa Bowman
Claire Brace
Hugo Brailsford
Angie Bray
Caroline Bray and
   Beni
Gill Brennand
Hannah Brickner
Gemma Bridges
Cate Brimble
   combe-Clark

Rebecca Broad
Kristian Brodie
Alexander Brook
Meg Brooke
Jenni Brooks
Beverley Brown
David Brown
Karon Brown
Kathleen Brown
Richard Brown
Sally Browning
Sian Brumpton
Catherine Bryer
Leslie Buck
Elaine Buckley
Sarah Bullock
Alison Bunce
Janet Bunker
Rachel Burch
Julie Burling
Donna-Marie
   Burnell
Christina C Burns
Jess Burns
Nicki Burns
Joanne Burrows
Jessica Burston
Jo Burt
Alex Burton-Keeble
Mary Bush
Rose Bygrave
Heather Byram
Axel and Zoe Byrne
   (in memory)
Ann & Ross Byrne +
   Pi, Max & Benny
Vivian Cafarella
Jennifer Calder

Michelle Calka
Judi Calow
Maggie Camp
Donatella Campbell
Rosanna Cantavella
Catherine Cargill
Amy Caroline
Caroline Carpenter
Karen Carpenter
Jonathan Carr
Liz Carr
Raechel Carroll
Lorrie Carse-wilen
Philippa Carter
Holly Cartlidge
Philippa Carty-
   Hornsby
Abigail Cast
Susan Catley
Stephanie Cave
Alex Cawley
Heather Cawte
Justin Cetinich
Kathryn Chabarek
Tamasine
   Chamberlain
Laura Chambers
Caroline Champin
Liz Chantler
Zoe Chapman
Sarah Chappell
Heather Chappelle
Lisa Charlesworth
Deanna Chavez
Gill Chedgey
Susan Chedgey
Paul Cheney
Rose Chernick

Nigel Denise
Chichester
Joan Childs
Rachel Chilton
Claire Choong
Lesley Christensen
Kirsten Christiansen
Valerie Christie
Linda Church
Amy Ciclaire
Lisa Claire
Jennifer Clapham
Adrian Clark
Heather Clark-
Evans
Lily Clarke
Mandy Clarke
Penne Clayton
Gill Clifford
Freyalyn Close-
Hainsworth
Lori Coates
Shannon
Andy Cochrane
Stevyn Colgan
Diane Collins
Marguerite Collins
Sally Collins
Trisha Connolly
Susanne Convery
Clare Coombes
Fiona Cooper
Dan Copeman
Jackie Copping
Sue Corden
Rosie Corlett
Ellie Cornell
Amanda Corp

Georgia Corrick
Anne Costigan
Sarah Cottam
Catherine Cottrell
Karen Coutts
Kati Cowen
Geoff Cox
Jo Cox
Louise Cox
Ann Crabbe
Melissa Crain
Sara Crane
Charlotte Crisp
Tessa Crocker
Esther Cropper
Nancy Crosby
Alasdair Cross
Rachel Cross
Vivienne Crossley
Neil Crosswell
Julia Croyden
Leah Culver-
Whitcomb
Michele Cumming
Pam Cummins
Anne Cunningham
Cush
Matthew d'Ancona
Beth Dallam
Patricia Daloni
Jackie Daly
Claire Daniells
Gimli Daniels
Elizabeth Darracott
Claire Davidson
Karen Davidson
Meryl Davies
Sharon Davies-

Patrick
Alice Davis
Ariella Davis
Catherine Davis
Laura Davis
Patrick Davis
Jeannie Davison
Alexandra Dawe
Rebecca Dawson
Annie de Bhal
Antony de
Heveningham
Celia Deakin
Frances Deaves
Joanne Deeming
Vicky Deighton
Nat Delaney
Conor Dempsey
Pamela Denison
Jill L Dent
Robin Denton
Albert Depetrillo
Emma Dermott
Heather Desserud
Suzie Dewey
Mark Diacono
Claire Dickson
Glenn Dietz
Christine Diorio
Zoë Donaldson
Rhona Donnelly
Catherine Dorrell
Marina Dorward
Jill Doubleday
Linda Doughty
Katy Driver
Miyako Dubois
Hilary Duffus

Sheila Dunn
Julie Dunne
Lucy Dunphy
Vivienne Dunstan
Amanda Durbin
Pene Durston
Thom Dyke
Karen Dyson
Simon Eardley
Rachel Easom
Christopher
    Easterbrook
Sarah Eden
James Edmonston
Patricia Edwards
Sharon Edwards
Eirlys Edwards-Behi
Tiril Thorshaug Eide
Deb Ekstrom
Esther Ellen
Tom Ellett
Debbie Elliott
Shaun Elliott
Ashley Elsdon
Elisabeth England
Kelly England
Ann Engler
Katie Enstone
Alex Epps
Dawn Erb
Raelene Ernst
Marina Etienne
Carol Evans
Isobel Evans
Karen Evans
Rachael Ewing
Christine Exley
Jeffrey Falconer

Shelley Fallows
Gina E. Fann
Sarah Faragher
Alessandra Farrell
Alison Farrell
Verity Ferguson
Peter Fermoy
Susannah Field
Erika Finch
Pamela Findlay
Finest Titloaf (and
    Oliver)
Anna Fisher
Julie Flanagan
Sorella Fleer
Joanne Fletcher
Fiona Floyd
Joanna Forbes
Christine Fosdal
Fi Fowkes
Gillian Foxcroft
Jane France
Nancy Franklin
Christine Fraser
Jacqueline Freeman
Jennifer Freitas
Liz Frost
Rebecca Frost
Simon Frost
Sherry Fuller
Rai Furniss-Greasley
Matthew Fuszard
Deborah Fyrth
Siobhan Gallagher
    Kent
Mel Gambier-Taylor
Mark Gamble
Pattie Gardet

to-Kuchma
Ian Gardiner
Emma Gardner
Laura Gardner
Nan Gardner
Rory Garforth
Christine Garret-
son-Persans
Sam Gawith
Clare Gee
Sally Geisel
Mark Gessner
Claire Gibney
Rebecca Gibson
Amber Gill
Laura Gill
Joanne Gillam
Richard Gillin
Lisa Gironda
Vivien Gledhill
Jayne Globe
GMarkC
Dave Goddard
Sierra Godfrey
Jennifer Godman
Leo Goldsmith
Katie Goodall
Rich Goodall
Susan Goodfellow
Mandy Gordon
Rachel Goswell
Toby Gould
Pat Gower
Natalie Graeff
Emma Graham
Tiffanni Grams
Peter Gray
Darrell Green

Hayley Green
Rebecca Greer
Laura Griffin
Judith Griffith
Louise Griffiths
Rachel Griffiths
Sharon Grimshaw
Helen Grimster
Claire Grinham
Julia Wagner Grover
Grumpy Craw
Juliana Grundy
Brenda Gurung
Rebecca Gusler
Anne Guy
Sara Habein
Julie Hadley
Beth Hale
Anna Hales
Kate Hall
Lizzie Hall
Fay Hallard
Marie Halova
Lauren Hamer
Stuart Hamilton
Sharon Hammond
Mary Hampton
Margaret Hand
Kate Hannaby
Cathy Hanson
Emma Hardy
Hilary Harley
Candy Harman
Lynda Harpe
Sue Harper
Rachel Harrington
Faith Harris
Fran Harrison

Ruby Harrison
Sharon T Harrison
Greg Harrop
Celia Hart
Jane Harvey
Kay Harvey
Julie Hastings
Luke Hatton
Emily Hawkins
Jackson Hays
Elspeth Head
Gillian Heaslip
Richard Hein
Katherine Helps
Cathy Henderson
Lynne Henderson
James Hendry
Mallory Henson
Elizabeth Henwood
Ben Herbert
Amanda Heslegrave
Anneka Hess
Diane Heward
Eve Hewlett-Booker
Anne Hiatt
Jan Hicks
Linda Hill
Rich Hill
Kayleigh Hillcoat
Carlien Hillebrink
Charlotte Hills
Ann Hiloski-Fowler
Emily Hine
Beth Hiscock
Kahana Ho
Jackie Hobbs
Becky Hodges
Susanna Hoffman

Jason Hold
    croft-Long
Rocki Lu Holder
Dianne Holland
Samantha Holland
Claire Holliss
Gilly Holmes
Holly Holmes
Kathryn Holt
Barbara Holten
Jacob Hoogland
Frances Hopkins
Pamela S. M.
    Hopkins
Geoffrey Horn
Clare Horne
Andy Horton
Peter Hoskin
Sophie Houston
Kathryn Howard
Clare Isobel Hughes
Crystal Hughes
Jennifer Hughes
Yvette Huijsman
Alison Hull
Sandy Humby
The Huntliffes &
    Lola the dog
    (aka pooface)
Shayne Husbands
Danie Hutchin
Claire Hutchinson
Gisele Huxley
Kay Hyde
Christine Ince
Josh Ingojo
Dagny Ingram
Hazel Ireland

Marie Irshad-
Nordgren
Anna Jackson
Jess Jackson
Judith Jackson
Pamela Jacobs
Sandra James
Elizabeth Jane
Floyd Janet
Marieke Jansen
Sarah Jarvis
Kim Jarvis &
Peter Taylor
Christine Jenner
Niki Jennings
Stinne Jensdotter
Lisa Jepson
Deborah Joachim
Rebecca Jobes
Gurney
Andrea Johnson
Vicki Johnson
Emma Johnston
Pauline Johnstone
Allison Joiner
Craig Jones
John Jones
Meghan Jones
Suzi Jones
Rolf Jordan
Alice Jorgensen
Sara Joseph
Melissa Joulwan
Mary Jowitt
Caroline Joyce
Andres Kabel
Lori Kasenter
Julie Kasperson

Jo Keeley
Karen Keene
Bridget Keener
Minna Kelland
Carolyn Kellogg
Gill Kelly
Teresa Kendall
Helen Kennedy
Denise Kennefick
Debbie, Graeme,
Rigby, Charlie &
Dudley Kerr
Mary Kersey
Rebecca Kershaw
Karin Kessels
Audrey Keszek
Dan Kieran
Ania Kierczynska
Stephanie Kilb
Peta Kilbane
Janet T King
Jon Kiphart
Jackie Kirkham
Mia & Reggie
Kitten
Kelsey Kittle
Ty Kittle
Ann Klimek
Alison Klose
Jules Knight
Korin Knight
Rachel Knightley
Mel Knott
Patricia Knott
Rick Koehler
Laurie Koerber
Sandra Kohls
Riek Koman

Ingrid Kornstad
Lidia Kuhivchak
Laurie Kutoroff
Dawn Lacey
Kevin Lack
Susan L Lacy
Leslie Lambert
Emma Lamerton
Peter Landers
Patty Langner
Teresa Langston
Joelle Lardi
Caldonia Larkin
Nicole Larkin
Phil Latham
Ronni Laurie
Vanessa Laurin
Terry Lavender
Delia Lavigne
Judith Lawless
Catherine Layne
Kim Le Patourel
Morgan Le Roy
Jim Leary
Capucine Lebreton
Claire Lee
Samm Lees
Esther Leeves
Liz Leigh
Alice Leiper
Kathryn Leng
Alison Lennie
Sandi Leonard
Catherine Lester
Jill Lethbridge
Helen Lever
Alex Levine
Beth Lewis

Helen Lewis
Katherine J. Lewis
Liz Lewis
Marian Lewis
Susan Lindon-Hall
Ian Lipthorpe
Katie Lister
David Livingston
Victoria Lloyd
Siân Lloyd-Pennell
Helen Looker
Catriona M. Low
Jennifer Lowe
Caroline Lucas
Rosalind Lucas
Jude Lucas-Mould
Helen Luker
Mrs Jackie Lynch
Josh M
Suzanne Richmond
    Maasland
Margo MacDonald
Penny Macdonald
Zoe Macdonald
Mara MacDougall
Karen Mace
Helen Mackenzie-
    Burrows
Russell Mackintosh
Laura Magnier
Nicki Maguire
Niamh Maher
Rebecca Major
Catherine Makin
Claire Mander
Alice Mannering
Laura Manners
Elliott Mannis

Keith Mantell
Tracey Mantrone
Anne Margerison
Charlotte Mark
Peter Marrs
Anne-Marie
    Marshall
Mary Martley
Catherine Mason
Jo Mason
Laura Mason
Louise Matchett
Suzanne Matrosov-
    Vruggink
Becca Mattingley
Vicky Maull
Joanne McBride
Cat McCabe
Laura McCarthy
Megan McCormick
Joel McCracken
Helen McElwee
Jane McEwan
Angela McGhin
Barbara McGonagle
Ann McGregor
Liz McGregor
Alison McIntyre
David McKean
Colleen McKenna
Vanessa McLaughlin
Cate Mclaurin
Fi McLoughlin
Mary McManus
Claire McMullen
Liz McNeil Grist
Leanna McPherson
Denise McSpadden

    & Freya the black
    cat
Melanie McVey
Bea Mehta
Barbara Joan Meier
Kate Menzies
Stacy Merrick
Holly Metcalf
Ali Middle
Elgiva Middleton
Mighty Oak &
    The ELM
Brian Miller
Eilidh Miller
Michelle Miller
Scott Millington
Chris Mills
David Minton
Laura Mitchell
John Mitchinson
Deena Mobbs
Sebastian Moitzheim
Richard Montagu
    Jennifer Montgomery
Kim Moody
Chris Moore
Emma Moore
Kristine Moore
Natalie Moore
Sarah Mooring
Sarah Moran
Trish Morgan
Jackie Morris
Mercy Morris
Katrina Moseley
Cathy Mossman
Florentina Mud
    shark

Donna Mugavero
Wendy Murguia
Claire Murphy
Ian Murphy
Clive Murray
Meg Murrell-
	Peloquin
Sheena Mushett
	Cole
Mel Mutter
Vanda Naden
Samantha Nasset
Carlo Navato
Tim Neville
Briony Newbold
Anne Newman
Caron Newman
Colleen Newton
Sarah Newton-Scott
Ducky Nguyen
Laura Niall
Valerie Niblett
Alicia Nicolson
Liz Nicolson
Andy Nikolas
Claire Nodder
Sarah Noone
Anita Norburn
Sheila North
Hugh Nowlan
Adele Nozedar
Brunna Nunes
Andrew Nunn
Liz & Ian
	O'Halloran
Mark O'Neill
Hannah O'Regan
Laura O'Hara Sibra

Rachel Oakes
Sarah Oates
Heather OBeirne
	Sandra Ober-
broeckling
Valerie Olsen
Linda Oostmeyer
Kylie Osborn
Vita Osborne
Deborah Owen
Kirsten Pairpoint
Pam Palmer
Sarah Palmer
Imogen Paradise
Lisa Parker
Catherine Parkin
Claire Parsons
Kevin Parsons
Soraya Pascoe
Karen Paton
Trish Paton
April Patrick
Adam R Patterson
Gill Patterson
Paul & Jess
Melanie Peake
Janice Pedersen
Ann Peet
Sally Pellow
Karie Penhaligon
Lisi Perner
Doris Peter
Sarah Peters
Sean Peters
Caroline Petit
Leslie Phelps
Michael Phythian
Chris Pickard

Lisa Piddington
Stephen Pieper
Karen F. Pierce
Bethany Pinches
Peter Pinkney
Tim Plester
Sarah Plumer
Jo Plumridge
Lucy Plunkett
Justin Pollard
Fernanda Pontes
Machado
Annette Poole
Jackie Poole
Kathryn Poole
Claire Poore
Robert Preece
Sally Preece
Catherine Prendergast
Virginia Preston
Mary Prevost
Laura Price
Arthur Prior
Stephen Procter
Catherine Prosser
Christie Punnett
Lisa Quattromini
Kate Quayle
Lisa Quigley
Melissa Quinn
Sue Radford
Helen Rainbow
Lucy Raine
Keith Ramsey
Tina Rashid
Laura Rathbone
Angela Rayson
Kerie Receveur

Ceoltoir Redman
Alison Rees
Lynn Reglar
Louise Reid
Vivienne Reid-
    Brown
Peg Reilly
Tamsin Reinsch
Steph Renaud
Tamar Resnick
Marie Reyes
Michelle Reynolds
Julie Richards
Laura Richmond
Ruth Richmond
Sarah Ridgway
Meryl Rimmer
Nicola Rimmer
Kerry Rini
Lucy Rix
Amanda Roberts
Catherine Roberts
Amanda Robertson
Norman Robinson
Spencer Robinson
Rachel Robison
Mike Rodriguez
Jane Roe
Valerie Roebuck
Susan Rollinson
Tom Roper
Sherry Ross
Matthew Rowell
Rhona Rowland
Helen Rule-Jones
Sue Rupp
Amy Ryall
Claire Ryan

S10 feeder
Karl Sabino
Katie Sajnog
Puskas Salts
Craig Sandison
Lyni Sargent
Sarah Savage
Sherri Savage
Jenni Schimmels
Julia Schlotel
Katharine Schopflin
Anna Schreiber
Chad Schrock
Lisa Sciberras
Jenni Scott
Sarah Scott
Alison Scruton
Jane Seager
Andrew Seaman
Jonathan Seaman
Lisa Search
Cora Seip
Sian Sellars
Emma Selwood
Karen Sem
Alasdair Semple
Beth Setters
Emma Seward
Laura Sewell
Belynda J. Shadoan
Mariese Shallard
Sharon
Victoria Sharratt
    McConnell
Iola Shaw
Jane-Anne Shaw
Matt Shaw
Tara K. Shepersky

Emmajane Sheppard
Josephine Sherwood
Jane Shillaker
Karen Shipway
Alison Shore
Wendy Shorter
Laura Simmonds
Melissa Sims
Joe Skade
Debbie Slater
Jane Slavin
Barendina Smedley
Bec Smith
Carolyn Smith
Claire Smith
Eleanor Smith
Fiona Katherine
    Smith
Hannah Smith
Helen Smith
Lan-Lan Smith
Libby Smith
Mairéad Smith
Michael Smith
Rosie Smith
Sarah Smith
Julia Snell
Michael Soares
Ingrid Christine
    Solberg
Yve Solbrekken
Murielle Solsikke
    Solheim
Roberta Solmundson
Julie Sorrell
Peter Souter
Anne Sowell
Kit Spahr

Caroline Sparks
Lyn Speakman
Maureen Kincaid
  Speller
Chris Spence
Rosslyn Spokes
Richard Stagg
Pam Stanier
Elizabeth Stanley
Hannah Stark
Sarah Steer
Angie Stegemann
Ros Stern
Ruth Stevens
Jason Stewart
Kristi Stewart
Beth Stites
Mary Stoicoiu
Shelagh Stoicoiu
Carmen Stone
Gwilym R Stone
Stephanie Strahan
Brigit Strawbridge
Duncan Strickland
Bridget Strugnell
Rachel Stubbs
Nina Stutler
Nadia Suchdev
Richard Sulley
Helen E Sunderland
Adam Sussman
Laurel Sutton
Cousin Sven
Claire Swain
Caroline Swan
Sweaty Witch Pants
Toni Swiffen
Jo Swift

Russell Swindle
Kirsty Syder
Angela Sykes
Ian Synge
Angie Tanner
Anna Tarnowski
Alison Taylor
Brigid Taylor
Dave Taylor
Georgette Taylor
Kay Taylor
Lynne Taylor
Siobhan Taylor
Sue Tett
Marthe Tholen
Dave & Jan Thomas
Donna Thomas
Lindsey Thomas
Sam Thomas
Andrea Thompson
Claire Thompson
Fern Thompson
Helen Thompson
Liz Thompson
Mary Ann Thompson
Lynne, Kylie, Donna
  & Shelley Thomson
Donna Tickner
Lynne Tidmarsh
Sarah Till-Vattier
Anka Tilley
Pernille Charlotte
  Tillisch
Adam Tinworth
Joanne Todd
Pippa Tolfts
Stacy Tomaszewski
Angela Townsend

Karen Trethewey
Kate Tudor
Liana Turner
Ruth Turner
Claira Turvey
Suzy Tweddle
Anita Uotinen
Sonja van Amelsfort
Anna van den Bosch
Brenda van Dinther
Sophie van Koevorden
Katja van Nus
Shane Van Veghel
Arianna Vander
  Houwen
Anne Vasey
Alexander Verkooijen
Sally Vince
Vivian Vincek
Paul Vincent
Rosalind Vincent
Alice Violett
Louise Vlach
Nicole Vlach
Ann "Teeting-
  Beastie" Voelkel
Leslie Wainger
Allyson Wake
Sarah Wakes
Karen Waldron
Claire Walker
Peter Walker
Stephen Walker
Sue Walker
Niki Walkey
Nick Walpole
Declan Walsh
Joolz Ward

Kezia Ward
Lee Ward
Sinead Ward
Matthew Wassell
Claire Watkins
Fran Watkins
Bj Watson
Rachel Watt
Catherine Watts
Waving Cloud
M. F. Webb
Lisa Webster
Julie Weller
Clair Wellsbury-Nye
Clancy Wendt
Jane Werry
Lyn West
Lucy Weston
Katy Wheatley
Mark Whitehead
Robert Whitelock
Miranda Whiting
Annalise Whittaker
Cassie Whittell
Carly Whyborn
Robin Wiggs
Anne-Marie Willard
Jullien
Linda Willars
Caroline Williams
Eileen Williams
Jenny Williams
Christopher James
Willis
Laura Willis
Rosamund Willis
  -Fear
Derek Wilson

Fiona Wilson
Kirsten Wilson
Tracey Wilson
Oliver Wilton
Camilla Winlo
Caroline Winter
Dawn Winter
Steve Winter
Anna Wittmann
Gretchen Woelfle
Kanina Wolff
Laiane Wolfsong
James K Wood
John Wood
Judith Wood
Peter Wood
Rebecca Wood
Joanna Woodhouse
Mark Woods
  ford-Dean
Elizabeth Wright
Melanie Wright
Rebecca Wyeth Fox
Jo Wynell-Mayow
Debbie Wythe
Theresa Yanchar
J L Yates
Stephanie Yates
Joanne Young
Lisa Young
Pam Young
Donna Zillmann
Birgit Zimmer-
mann-Nowak